You and Me, Babe

Chuck Barris

HARPER'S MAGAZINE PRESS
Published in Association with Harper & Row
New York

YOU AND ME, BABE. Copyright © 1974 by Chuck Barris Productions, Inc. All rights reserved. Printed in the United States of America. No part of this book may be used or reproduced in any manner whatsoever without written permission except in the case of brief quotations embodied in critical articles and reviews. For information address Harper & Row, Publishers, Inc., 10 East 53rd Street, New York, N.Y. 10022. Published simultaneously in Canada by Fitzhenry & Whiteside Limited, Toronto.

Designed by Gloria Adelson

Library of Congress Cataloging in Publication Data
Barris, Chuck.
  You and me, babe.
  A novel.
  I. Title.
PZ4.B2766Yo   [PS3552.A7367]   813'.5'4   73–17635
ISBN 0–06–120342–4

To Della, whom I love more than
anybody in the whole world

Part 1

*W*e met when I was twenty and Sammy was fourteen. . . . She was fat, wore braces, and was a friend of my sister Geraldine, who was fat and wore braces. Sammy almost always wore her hair in pigtails. I remember that distinctly.

I may have met Sammy when she was younger. She and my sister went to summer camp together from the time they were eight years old until they were thirteen. My father couldn't really afford to send my sister to an exclusive girls' camp like the one Sammy went to, but he sent her anyway.

Still, the moment I truly remember seeing Sammy first was when she was fourteen and I found her in my bedroom.

"What's your name?" I asked.

"Sammy," she answered. "Actually my full name is Samantha Jane Wilkerson, but everybody calls me Sammy."

"Well, Samantha Jane Wilkerson, get your ass out of my bedroom! Wasn't the door closed? Doesn't a closed door mean keep out? Do me a favor, Samantha. When you see my bedroom door closed, stay out. Understand?"

"Yes, I understand," she said, and started to leave.

"Hey!" I hollered.

She stopped and looked at me.

"When the door's *open*, stay out."

"Fine," said Samantha Jane Wilkerson, and then she walked away.

"Just keep out of my room!" I yelled again as she went downstairs. In those days I hated my sister's friends almost as much as I hated my sister.

Samantha Jane Wilkerson told my sister I said the word "ass," my sister told my mother, and my mother came to my room to give me her periodic lecture on how I shouldn't be so awful to my sister *and* my sister's friends. I knew she was mad because she talked with her hands on her hips. She said that I could use a little dignity and manners, and that I should show my sister, and her friends, some respect.

"Sometimes your behavior shocks me, Tommy Christian. You're a grown man of twenty, for God's sake. And besides, if you have to be rude to your sister's friends, pick on somebody else, but be nice to Samantha. She's probably the only decent friend Geraldine has."

My mother was beautiful then. It was before my father had his stroke, and we lost what little money we had, and my mother had to go to work. When I was twenty my mother looked thirty. She was petite, very much alive, and very impressed with money. Her family had it before the crash, and she never got over losing it, although she said she did.

"And she's very rich," continued my mother. "Samantha Wilkerson just happens to be one of the richest girls in New York."

"So?"

"So she's the type of friend your sister should cultivate. Samantha is a lot more important to Geraldine than all of her other ninny friends combined. Geraldine could meet a lot of interesting boys through Samantha."

"You mean a lot of *rich* boys," I said with a sneer.

"Right," said my mother. "A lot of rich boys. Is there anything wrong with that? You make it sound like having money is the worst thing in the world. Just remember what Groucho Marx said."

"What *did* Groucho Marx say?"

"He said, 'I've been rich and I've been poor, and rich is better.' " And then my mother walked out of my room.

"Just keep my fat sister and her fat friends away from me!" I shouted, so that everybody in the house could hear.

Between the ages of fourteen and seventeen, my sister Geraldine became beautiful, sophisticated, and fun to be with.

She also became my best friend.

There was something totally illogical about Geraldine, which was probably one of the reasons I grew to love her as much as I did. Another reason was her ability to drive my parents crazy.

"You know," my mother would say to her, "it's just as easy to meet rich friends as it is poor ones."

"Bullshit, Ma. And do me a favor. Save your materialistic crap for Tommy."

"Honestly, Geraldine, the way you've taken to cursing. You're a lady in every respect, except the way you curse, and I truly think—"

"Besides," interrupted my sister, "you know what Groucho Marx said. He said, 'If you marry for money, you *pay* for it.' "

"He didn't say that."

"Well, he should have," said my sister.

Geraldine was seventeen when she married Harrison T. Bartlett III. Her husband's nickname was H.T. I couldn't believe his name, and I couldn't stand his nickname, but I liked him.

H.T. was twenty-four, a year older than me, when he married Geraldine. He was tall, and not very good-looking. But he was warm, affectionate, very much in love with my sister, and very rich.

My sister Geraldine met Harrison T. Bartlett III at a party at Samantha Wilkerson's house.

"See," said my mother. "Wasn't I right when I told your sister that it was just as easy to meet rich friends as it was poor ones?"

"Aw, come on, Ma," I begged, "please get off my back with this money thing you have."

"Well, just promise me you'll think about it," said my mother.

I promised, just to shut her up.

When I was twenty-four I left our home in Queens and moved to Manhattan. Of all the apartments available for renting on the East Side of New York, mine was one of the cheapest. It was also one of the worst. It was on the top floor of a five-story walk-up near the corner of Fortieth Street and Third Avenue. The apartment was freezing in the winter and suffocating in the summer. There was always a drunken tramp either passed out in the vestibule or pissing on it, and for one reason or another, all the itinerants in the neighborhood rang my door buzzer, twenty-four hours a day.

The apartment had a living room with a kitchenette, a bathroom, a bedroom, several rats, and hundreds of cockroaches, but no furniture of any kind, except a broken, shredded bamboo curtain that tried to hide the kitchenette. The curtain didn't go up *or* down. It just hung at an angle from two rusty hooks, its pull cord hopelessly tangled in its slats.

Slowly but surely, I added furniture that was equally devastated: a cot purchased at an army-navy store, two wobbly and scratched end tables a neighbor had thrown away, a lamp, and an alarm clock. The apartment was depressing but it was mine, and that was about all I could say for it.

One Saturday morning I woke up, looked around my crummy walk-up, and realized it was my birthday. I called my sister and told her.

"Well, get your ass up here then," she hollered. "Besides wishing you a happy birthday, I want to hear what's been happening, and anyway, you haven't been formally introduced to your first official nephew."

"Okay," I said. "I'll grab the first train I can get."

"By the way," continued my sister, "you'll have to sleep on the couch. I have a house guest for the weekend."

"That's okay, too," I said. "Is it anybody I know?"

"Yes, you know her. She's one of my fat friends you used to bitch about to Mother."

"Who?"

"Sammy Wilkerson."

Looking out of train windows has the same effect on me as watching a fire in a fireplace. I think about things.

I thought about my father.

The poor bastard always smelled like feet.

Being a chiropodist wasn't an easy way to make a living. There just weren't enough corns and bunions around to make ends meet.

Money.

Without it you had to live in a cheap walk-up and step in some vagrant's piss first thing in the morning. Without it you had to work in a Doubleday bookstore, constantly flattering effeminate floor managers so they didn't report you for punching out five minutes early at the end of the day.

Maybe my mother was right. I've been rich and I've been poor, and rich is better.

The conductor yelled, "Westport!"

I stepped off the train, kissed my sister, and said hello to her friend, Samantha Jane Wilkerson, one of the richest girls in America.

"You look great, Sammy," I said. "You really do."

"Thank you," she said. "You don't."

She was right. I didn't. I hadn't shaved, and I looked scruffy.

"You look like a goddamn bum," said my sister. "When's the last time you had a bath and a good hot meal?"

"I can't remember," I said.

7

"Well, happy birthday anyway," said my sister.

"Yes, happy birthday," said Samantha Jane Wilkerson.

Geraldine's house was magnificent. It was big, white, and rambling, and very French. It had a long tree-lined driveway that curled up to its front door, and inside were lots of fireplaces, and soft, comfortable armchairs and couches.

Harrison, Geraldine's husband, gave me a bear hug and slapped a Bloody Mary into my hand. Then the two of them forced me to see their baby before I did anything else. Its name was Jason, and it was wrinkled and ugly.

Geraldine giggled. She said, "Isn't he cute?"

"Yes," I lied, "it's adorable."

"He's not an *it!* He's a *he,*" she said, miffed.

Everyone stood around the crib beaming at the little prune. I stole a look at Sammy and caught her looking at me.

"How old are you now, Samantha?" I asked.

"Eighteen. How old are *you* now?"

"Twenty-four," I answered. "You know, the last time I saw you, you were—"

"Fourteen."

Sammy and I went downstairs.

"Do you remember the last thing you said to me?" she asked.

"No."

"You told me to get my fat ass out of your room, and to stay out."

"That's hard to believe."

"I've got witnesses," said Samantha Jane Wilkerson.

Later that day, I soaked in a hot bath and thought about Sammy. She didn't wear braces anymore, and she wasn't fat. But she was still a little chubby, and she used too much makeup to suit me.

Anyway, she *does* have a good personality, and a good sense of humor, I said to myself, and that's important. And she had a great smile, and big beautiful brown eyes. But one of those big beautiful brown eyes was supposed to have a nervous twitch in it. I remembered my sister saying something about that. And I thought Geraldine also told me that Sammy had asthma.

So what? She dressed great, and I understood her father gave her the first Chevrolet Corvette in Greenwich, Connecticut. But didn't my sister once tell me that Sammy drank a lot, and that she kept a bottle of vodka in her closet?

That night I took Sammy to the movies.

I bought a box of Goobers, some popcorn, and a Pepsi. Sammy didn't want anything. As soon as we were seated, Sammy had her hand in my popcorn and was asking for a Goober or two.

"I never start eating my candy until the main feature begins," I said, a bit peeved.

"You're not serious?"

"Extremely."

"Then that's *your* problem," she said, reaching for the popcorn again.

I held the box off to one side.

She looked at me and laughed. Her left eye was twitching. It was the first time I noticed it.

"I don't think I'm going to like you," she said. "You're greedy."

She ate most of my popcorn, almost all of my Goobers, and never handed me back my Pepsi.

After the movie, we went to a restaurant for a snack. I ordered pie and ice cream, and a glass of milk. Sammy wanted a vodka and tonic. She finished it before my pie and ice cream came, and ordered a second one.

Sammy fingered the ice in her empty glass. Without looking up, she said, "When I was fourteen and you threw me out of your room, did you ever think you would try and get me drunk at the Blue Bell Inn?"

I didn't know where to begin answering that question.

By the time we got home, everyone had gone to sleep. Sammy

and I made some instant coffee and drank it in the kitchen. We talked for hours. I told Sammy my dream of becoming a writer. I explained how I intended to give myself a year at it, and if things didn't happen, if nothing I wrote was published in that time, I was still young enough to get a job and become president of a big company. I described my ambitions and laid out my plans for the future, making some of it up as I went along. I noticed happily that Sammy listened eagerly to every word I said.

"It sounds exciting," she said when I finished. "I know you'll be a success. I can just tell."

I couldn't get over how easy it was to carry on a conversation with Samantha. I thought heiresses would be tough to talk to. I had a harder time thinking of things to say to the secretaries I dated in New York than to Samantha Jane Wilkerson, a member of the family that owned the American Steel Corporation. Like my mother said, it's just as easy to meet rich girls as it is poor ones.

Somewhere around four in the morning Sammy stretched and said, "I think you're interesting as all get-out, but I'm exhausted." She stood up, said good night, and went to her room.

I stayed in the kitchen and reviewed our conversation. I had impressed Samantha. There was no doubt about that. I wasn't like her run-of-the-mill boyfriends. It was obvious that Sammy was bored with the social dandies she had been used to dating. I was different. I was ambitious and colorful, and had a charisma that excited her. And she was rich and bored, and vulnerable.

I stared into my empty coffee cup and decided right then and there to strike while the iron was hot. "Yes, sir," I said to the refrigerator. "I've never been rich, but I've been poor, and I'll just bet rich is better."

I tiptoed upstairs and knocked on Sammy's door.

"Sammy," I whispered.

There was no answer.

"Sammy," I said, a little louder.

"Yes," she answered.

"Can I come in? I've got something I'd like to tell you."

"Uh-huh."

I opened the door and stepped into the room. Samantha came out of the bathroom brushing her teeth. Her mouth was full of foam.

"Sammy," I said.

"Yes," she answered.

"I've got something I want to tell you."

"Okay," she said, still brushing her teeth.

"Sammy."

"Yes."

"Sammy, I'm going to marry you!"

She went back to the bathroom and continued brushing her teeth. I stood there like a damn fool.

In a few minutes she came out, wiping her mouth with a towel.

"I have a boyfriend," she said, sitting down on the edge of the bed. "He's in medical school in Boston. He's up there this weekend studying for his finals. My parents are in Saratoga Springs, and my brother is in Scottsdale, Arizona, for the weekend. That's why I'm staying here with Geraldine. I didn't want to be home alone. It's nice that you want to marry me, but I don't want to marry you. And if you remember correctly, both a closed door *and* an open door mean keep out, so get your skinny ass the hell out of my room so I can get some sleep."

I went back to the kitchen and made myself another cup of coffee. I drank it and waited for the sun to come up. It never did. It rained that day.

Two weeks later my father almost died.

He had a stroke. His right side was totally paralyzed and he couldn't talk. For the next three years he would be an invalid who had to be dressed and fed and taken to the bathroom. His stroke would leave him and my mother penniless.

11

"Why, Ma?" I asked.

"Because your father never believed in sickness, and therefore he never believed in insurance."

"Why didn't you say something to him?"

"I just found out this week. He never told me."

"How much is in the bank?"

"Very little. Apparently your father owes more than he has."

While my father was in the hospital, I closed up his office. I sold all of his instruments and equipment at a terrible loss to ratty little men who converged on me from out of nowhere. I gave the money to my mother to help pay some of my father's mammoth medical bills.

It wasn't enough.

We had to sell our row house in Queens.

My mother took my father and moved in with her parents, in their small apartment on the corner of Broadway and Eighty-third Street. Each month my sister would send my mother as much money as she could. I couldn't afford to give my mother a cent.

Money.

"It's a pain in the ass without it," said the drunk sitting next to me on the subway. "You don't have to be rich to be happy, young man, but it sure helps." He slapped my leg and asked me if I wanted to read his *New York Times*.

I saw a picture of Samantha Jane Wilkerson in the drunk's paper. She and her parents were standing in the winners' circle of some race track. One of the family's thoroughbreds had a wreath of red roses around its neck.

Sammy looked cute.

"Your apartment's a shithouse," said my sister.

"I know."

"Well, *do* something about it."

"What?" I asked.

"Anything!"

My sister cleaned the dishes and tried to fix the bamboo curtain before we went to Downey's. Every time my sister came to New York we would go to Downey's and drink beer and talk for hours.

"I tell H.T. that I have to go to New York and buy an entire new wardrobe, and he's so proud of me."

"For what?" I asked.

"For coming home without buying anything. He thinks I have a great respect for money. He doesn't know that I'd rather piss away the day drinking beer with my half-wit brother."

"I can't believe it," I said.

"Believe what?"

"I can't believe that I like you as much as I do."

"Oh, balls. I'm the best thing that ever happened to you."

"You know something, Geraldine, you *do* curse too much."

"Up yours!" said my sister. "Anyway, how's your love life?"

"Lousy." And it was, in a way.

That week I was dating a dumb blonde named Connie. She was also a clerk at the Doubleday bookstore, and every time we talked at any length, I wondered who her references were.

Before Connie there had been Mavis. She was a sloe-eyed Georgia peach who believed in segregation and free love.

"That's a fantastic combination, if you think about it," I told my sister.

Before Mavis, there was the girl who kept panting, "Tell me what you like. Tell me what you like." And before her, there was the girl who told me what *she* liked. And before her was the girl who informed me that she rated all her lovers, and that I was her third named Tommy. And before her was the girl who said, "God, what's wrong with me tonight?" And before her was the girl who said, "What's wrong with you tonight?" And before her was someone else, and before her there was someone else.

"You know what I can't stand, Geraldine?"

"What?"

"Dating! It's a lousy institution. I hate calling up girls to get turned down and when I *do* get lucky, they always live on the other side of town. I'm going broke on cab fares. I'm also getting tired of having to make clever conversation and wondering whether I'm dressed right. I'm fed up with meeting girls' room-mates, and knowing the girl can't wait to get back to her apartment so that she and her cute little roomies can pick me apart and laugh at all the smart and witty things I said. I'm getting sick and tired of going numb with fear when a pimple breaks out on my forehead. You know what? Dating's a pain in the ass."

"Why don't you stay home and read a good book?" asked my sister.

"It's too lonely."

Seven months after my father got out of the hospital, he came to visit me. He stayed a week. It felt like a year. I couldn't wait until he left. It wasn't that he was trouble. It was that my father was so depressing. He would sit in the one chair I had and look out of my window all day and all night.

Most of the time we would eat our meals out. Once in a while, I would get something from the delicatessen and bring it back to my apartment. Sometimes my father would go to the store with me. One time I heard him trying to tell the counterman something. My father could hardly talk, and the waiter wasn't even paying any attention to him.

My father was trying to say, "I was a chiropodist. I was a chiropodist." A hopeless cripple, leaning on a cane, his right arm hanging dead, slobbering out of the side of his mouth to a stupid short-order cook, "I was a chiropodist."

I was crying when I led him out of the store, but I didn't let him see me.

"How do you feel?" asked my sister on the telephone.

"I feel fine."

"Good. Will you do me a favor?"

"Maybe. What?"

"Take a friend of mine to a party. I'll pay your train fare back and forth."

"Which friend?" I asked.

"Bernice Chapman."

"I don't know her, do I?"

"No. She's adorable. She's really a good time. I wouldn't screw you up, would I?"

"How come she can't get a date? Is she a beast or something?"

"Oh, come off it," said my sister. "She has a boyfriend, but he can't get down from school. And it's a big party. She doesn't want to miss it. Besides, it's a good chance for you to meet some new faces, too. It could be the party of the year. You'll have fun, I promise, and there's no complications. Please."

"Okay."

"Great! You're a doll!" said my sister. "Bye, Tommy."

"*Hey!*" I hollered.

"What?" asked my sister, sighing heavily.

"Who's throwing this big exciting party of the year that Bernice what's-her-name can't miss?"

"Sammy Wilkerson."

The Wilkerson mansion was impressive, to say the least. The house was a red brick affair that stretched for an acre. It stood on the corner of a stately suburban street that wound pavementless past an endless row of estates.

A long half-moon driveway rolled by the mansion's front door. Cars, standing bumper to bumper, followed the curve of the driveway from one end to the other. They were not the cars of the elderly rich: the Cadillacs, Lincolns, and Rolls-Royces. These were the Corvettes, little Mercedeses, and Porsche convertibles of the children of the elderly rich.

My sister loaned me a car, which I had to park four blocks away. It was okay, though. Bernice Chapman didn't mind the walk.

"Walking's good for you," she said.

Bernice Chapman looked like a Bernice Chapman. I think my sister lied about a boyfriend that couldn't get down from school, but that was all right. Bernice Chapman was trying hard, and I think she was as uneasy as I was about going inside the Wilkerson house.

"Are you a friend of Ted's?" she asked.

"No. I'm a friend of Samantha's."

"Oh."

"Are you a friend of Samantha's, too?" I asked.

"Yes."

"A good friend?"

"No," sighed Bernice Chapman, "just a *mezzo e mezzo* friend. Are you a good friend of Samantha's?"

"Nope. Just *mezzo e mezzo,* too."

"Do you like the Wilkersons?" asked Bernice Chapman.

"No. Do you?"

"Not at all," said Bernice Chapman, giggling.

Bernice Chapman and I looked at each other warmly, and as we approached the doorway, I think we both took a deep breath.

The party was a bore. It seemed to be a gathering of the Connecticut elite, and being the son of a poor, crippled ex-chiropodist, I wasn't what you might call a thrill a minute for the female social climbers at the ball.

"What's your father do?" asked Bernice Chapman.

"He's an archduke," I said.

"He is *not* an archduke," said my sister, dragging her husband Harrison by his arm through the crowd to where we were standing. "He's a chiropodist, and he's the best goddamn chiropodist in the whole world. How do you two like the party?"

"It's thrilling," I said.

Around midnight I went upstairs to go to the bathroom. Afterward, I sneaked a look around and found Sammy's bedroom. It was very feminine, but very bare. There were hardly any mementos in the room. The only exceptions were a guitar, and a small

16

framed picture on her dresser of a fat-faced fop who had to be her boyfriend. I took the guitar, sat down on her bed, and sang some songs to myself.

"You play the guitar, I see," said Samantha Jane Wilkerson. She was standing in the doorway. I don't know how long she had been standing there.

"Not very well," I said.

"I think you play well."

"Really?"

"Yes, really," she said, and sat down on the bed next to me.

I strummed some more, and not taking my eyes off my fingers, I said, "How have you been?"

"Fine. And yourself?"

"Fine."

"How's your father?" she asked. "I heard he's been very sick."

"Yes, he has," I said. "He had a pretty bad stroke. He's paralyzed and he can hardly talk. It's sad because he was such an energetic man."

"I'm sorry to hear that," she said.

"Oh, it could be worse, I guess. He could be dead. At least we can still hug and kiss him a lot."

I strummed some more.

Sammy clasped her hands between her knees.

"How's your love life?" she asked.

"How's my what?"

"Your love life. You don't mind me asking, do you?"

"No. I just didn't think it mattered to you *what* my love life was like."

"Oh, I don't lose a hell of a lot of sleep over it," she said. "I was just curious. You're getting to be kind of an old fart and I thought you'd be getting married by now."

"I never really thought of myself as an old fart."

"You *are* twenty-six or twenty-seven, aren't you?" she said.

"Twenty-five."

"Okay, twenty-five. In five years you'll be thirty! Remember, I'm still a teen-ager."

"My love life's been fine," I said.

"Good."

"And speaking of love lives, how's your fiancé?" I asked. "I can see by his picture on your dresser that you go for the fat type."

"That picture on my dresser," said Sammy, "is my brother, who happens to be fat. My fiancé is slim and handsome. Do you know that I had a crush on you when I was fourteen? And do you know that when you threw me out of your bedroom you almost broke my heart?"

"I didn't know that," I said. I played some more chords on Sammy's guitar. "If you had such a crush on me, then how come you didn't marry me when I asked you to a year ago?"

"Because I got over my crush when I was fifteen," she replied. "Besides, that was a stupid grandstand play you were pulling. I don't like showboats. And how come you're in my bedroom?"

I never had a chance to answer. Someone said, "So *there* you are. I've been looking all over for you." He was slim and handsome, and he wore a tuxedo.

"Well, you found me," said Sammy indifferently. She walked over to a chest of drawers, opened one, took out a half-empty bottle of vodka, and poured some into a glass she'd brought to her room.

"The party's busting up," said the guy in the tux, "and we're all going to the club. We've been waiting for you. Your brother's mad as hell."

"He'll get over it," Sammy said. She turned and looked at me. "Tommy, I'd like you to meet George Carruthers Larkspur, Jr. His friends call him Skip. Skip, this is Tommy Christian. Tommy's an old fart that I used to have a crush on when I was fourteen. Don't worry about it, though. I got over it when I was fifteen."

Samantha Jane Wilkerson and George "Skip" Larkspur, Jr., left me sitting there with Sammy's guitar on my lap.

18

I found Bernice Chapman, took her home, returned my sister's car to her house, walked to the station, and grabbed a milk train to New York.

So much for the party of the year.

The next morning the phone rang and rang and rang. By the time I woke up and grabbed the receiver, the caller had hung up. I cursed and looked at the alarm clock. It was eight-thirty in the goddamn morning. I fell back into my pillow and pulled the covers over my head.

The phone started ringing again.

I answered it.

"Who the *hell* is this?" I growled.

"Sammy Wilkerson," said the voice.

We met at the Plaza Hotel in front of the Palm Court, at noon. I told her that I was sorry I yelled at her when she called.

"It's okay," she said. "I'm getting used to it. You've been yelling at me since I was fourteen."

We walked up Fifty-ninth Street to Rumpelmayer's and had brunch.

"What a nice surprise," I said. "What would George 'Skip' Larkspur, Jr., do if he knew we were meeting clandestinely in New York?"

"In simple terms?" asked Sammy.

"In simple terms."

"He'd die."

After brunch we took a walk through Central Park. It was a beautiful Sunday, and I felt good.

"Now that I think of it," I told Sammy, "it was pretty gutsy of you to visit my sister all the years that you did. Your parents don't seem the type that would be happy to have their one and only daughter bumming around with a poor chiropodist's kid."

"Maybe that's why I bummed around with a poor chiropodist's kid. I loved being around your family. There was always so much love in your house. You may not have had a lot of money, but there sure was a hell of a lot of hugs and kisses being spread around the place. Even when you hollered at Geraldine I could tell you loved her. Anyway, Geraldine is a wonderful person, and we both had a lot in common when we were kids. We both were fat and wore braces. And besides, like I said, I had a crush on you."

"Why?" I asked.

"Because you were rough and tough, ungrammatical, uncouth, and just plain different from the smooth, boring friends of my brothers. I used to actually dream of you putting the standard elopement ladder under my window and whisking me away from that God-awful penitentiary that I live in, to a little candy-coated gingerbread house where the two of us would live happily ever after. Do you live in a little candy-coated gingerbread house now?"

"Not exactly."

Sammy laughed and took my hand in hers. She walked me over to a vendor who had a pushcart with an orange and blue umbrella, and ordered a hot dog and a chocolate drink.

"We just had brunch," I said.

"Still greedy as ever," she said. "Don't worry. I'll pay for it."

I bought two hot dogs and two chocolate drinks, and we ate them sitting on a bench near the zoo. While we ate, Sammy asked me if I would take her to see the gorillas.

"Did you know," said Sammy, "that the mother monkey is the most protective and loving mother in the entire animal kingdom?"

"That bit of knowledge doesn't move me a hell of a lot," I said.

"It would if you were a baby monkey."

When we finished eating, I took Sammy to see the gorillas. One, an enormous female named Susie, looked directly at us for a few minutes, then went back to diligently picking nits out of her baby's scalp. The baby gorilla hung onto his mother's arm and nuzzled its head into her chest. Every now and then, Susie would kiss her baby on the top of its head and pat its back. Once in a while, the baby gorilla would run off to swing on a bar or look at people. Susie never took her eyes off him. When the baby came back, Susie would push it away, pretending she didn't want any part of her son. The little baby knew it was a game, and at times I could have sworn it smiled.

It was obviously a newborn baby because Susie's breasts were enormous. They hung down to her stomach. Whenever the baby gorilla was bored, it would burrow into its mother's lap and suckle on one of her great breasts. Sometimes it would bite too hard and Susie would smack it. The baby would look up into Susie's eyes, and the look between the two of them was pure love. After a few seconds the baby would go back to his suckling, Susie's arms would tighten around him, and she would look down adoringly at her child.

We watched Susie the gorilla for almost an hour. Sammy was mesmerized. She kept up a steady stream of sighs.

"Isn't it lovely?" she said. "Isn't it absolutely lovely?"

We took a bus to Washington Square.

"I hope you don't mind taking a bus," I said.

"Oh, come off it, Thomas."

"What's with this Thomas stuff?" I asked.

"Tommy reminds me of Skip, and Rocky. Names like that," she said.

"What's wrong with Skip?"

"Nothing," said Sammy, "if you like tall and handsome social catches."

"Don't you like tall and handsome social catches?" I asked.

"No," she answered. "Besides, George Carruthers Larkspur, Jr., is too meticulous. He's the kind that makes sure his nose is clean before he goes to the dentist."

We watched a basketball game in a playground and looked at some art hanging from a chain-link fence. We sat outside at O.

Henry's and drank mugs of beer and talked about the two of us.

"I want to write short stories," I said, "and books and plays, and maybe even a movie. If a book I wrote was ever published, or a play of mine performed, I'd go out of my mind. I really would."

"What have you written so far?" she asked.

"Just some short stories. Nothing important."

"Why haven't you written something important?"

"Because I haven't," I answered. "I guess it's because I've been putting it off. I have a novel in the back of my head that I've wanted to write, but I just keep putting it off."

"You better cut it out," she said.

"Cut *what* out?"

"Cut out putting it off. Remember, an old fart only becomes an older fart."

"Very funny," I said.

We browsed in a Marboro bookstore. When we walked out, Sammy handed me a package. She had bought me a book behind my back. It was called *Writing for Fun and Profit.*

We walked through Washington Square.

"I'm not very domestic," she said. "I can only cook omelets and steak, and I can hardly sew. I always stick myself with the needle."

"So?"

"So I'm glad I told you now, before it became embarrassing."

"Why?"

"Because you have two buttons that are about to fall off your sports coat, and I'll be goddamned if I'm going to bleed to death trying to sew them back on."

I asked her if she had ever heard of a thimble.

"A what?" she answered.

"You mean to tell me you never—"

"Of *course* I know what a thimble is. Every girl knows what a thimble is from the time they're a child. You use a thimble to take a hot pot out of the stove."

22

I wasn't sure she was kidding.

We went to a flea market. I bought Sammy a tattered cookbook and an ornate antique thimble.

"You practice your cooking and sewing," I said, "and I'll start writing my novel. Is that a deal?"

"It's a deal."

We had dinner at Mimi's, a small restaurant on East Fifty-third Street. Mimi was a fat Italian who would argue with his waiters in front of the customers, but neither the waiters nor the customers would pay any attention to him.

There was also an old black gentleman named Jack, who played the piano there. Everybody called him Jack-the-Piano-Player. Just half the keys on Jack-the-Piano-Player's piano worked, and Jack could only play five or six songs, which he played over and over again, badly. Between Mimi and Jack-the-Piano-Player, nobody was ever bored.

"I love this place," Sammy said.

"I'm glad."

Sammy leaned across the table and held my hand. She looked at me and said, "I've had a marvelous day with you. Thank you for showing me Thomas's New York. I loved the places you took me to, and most of all I loved listening to you talk. You have so much enthusiasm and love of life in you. It just bubbles out in everything you say."

"I bubble?"

"And you're not dull," said Sammy.

"Am I handsome?"

"No. But you're cute."

"I'm cute?"

"And unpredictable," Sammy added. "My brother, and his friends, and just about all the guys I've ever dated, are totally predictable. I can tell you exactly what's in store for them. Would you like to know?"

"Yes," I answered. What else was I going to say?

"Okay. First of all, they'll all go into their fathers' businesses, or join their fathers' law firms. Then they'll all belong to their fathers' country clubs, where they'll promptly cheat on their vapid little wives. Next they'll all inherit their fathers' box seats at the track, and lose a lot of their fathers' money, which they'll all also inherit. And when they die, they'll all be buried in their fathers' crypts, and that'll be that."

"Not me," I chirped.

"I know," she answered, and sneezed on my arm.

In the cab going to the train station, I told Sammy that I loved her. It took a lot of squeezing to get it out, but I said it. She smiled and we stared into each other's eyes for an amazingly long time. Then she told me she had asthma.

"So what?"

"So plenty. You haven't seen me when I have an asthma attack. It's terrible. I have to carry an atomizer in my purse." She showed me the atomizer. "I have to jam this God-awful thing down my throat and pump like hell. I've had attacks all my life, and each one still scares me to death. It's a big pain, but there's nothing I can do about it."

"Who cares?" I said cheerfully, but suddenly I cared.

When we got to the train station, I kissed Sammy good-bye and took a bus back to my apartment.

She's not worth it, I said to myself. A nineteen-year-old drunk with a twitching eye and asthma. I don't care how much money she has; who wants to marry a drunk with a twitching eye and asthma? And besides, like Geraldine used to say, if you marry for money, you pay for it.

Later that night I was lying in bed when the phone rang. I answered it, and Sammy said hello.

"Hi ya, Sammy."

"I just wanted to tell you again that I had a lovely time to-day."

"I'm glad," I said, with all the enthusiasm I could muster.

"See you next weekend?" she asked.

"Absolutely."

"Let me know what train you're taking, and I'll pick you up at the station."

"Okay."

"Do you still love me?" she asked.

"Yes."

"That's good, because I think I love you, too. Good night, Thomas."

"Good night, Sammy."

I put the phone down and fell back on my pillow.

"Who was that?" asked Bunny Winters, a pretty little redhead who had propped herself up on one elbow, and was wondering whether she should be mad or not.

"Nobody," I said, pulling Bunny down off her elbow. "It was just a guy who used to work with me at Doubleday's. Now where were we?"

"You know where we were," said Bunny Winters.

We were having a heat wave in New York. Everyone seemed either irritable or lethargic. I was both when I left my apartment to meet my sister and my mother at Downey's for dinner. It was Geraldine's treat.

"Hurry up and marry Sammy," said my sister, when we were seated. "I'm getting tired of carrying you two poverty cases on my back."

"Good thought," said my mother. "When *are* you going to marry Sammy?"

"How do you two know that Samantha Jane Wilkerson wants to marry *me?*" I asked.

"Listen," said my sister. "You could charm the balls off a cobra if you wanted to."

"Honestly, Geraldine—" began my mother.

"Anyway," I interrupted, "are you sure you want me to get mixed up with an asthmatic drunk?"

25

"Oh, for Christ sake," said my sister. "Sammy's not a drunk, you ass."

"Will you *please* watch your language, Geraldine," said my mother. "Tommy, will you talk to your sister about her language."

"Listen, Geraldine," I said. "It was *you* who told me that Sammy keeps a bottle of gin in her closet."

"It was only a rumor," said my sister. "Nothing but a goddamn rumor."

"Like hell it was! It's the goddamn truth! I saw it myself, except she doesn't keep the bottle in her closet; she keeps it in her dresser. And it's not gin; it's vodka!"

"She *does!*" said my sister.

"Yes, she does."

My sister slumped back in her chair.

"So what?" said my mother. "So what if she has a bottle of vodka in her dresser? Maybe she's unhappy. She's certainly not an alcoholic. I've never seen her drunk."

"You've never dated her, Ma."

"Listen, Tommy," said my mother. "Let me tell you something. First of all, nine out of ten cases of asthma are supposed to be psychosomatic. And Sammy's asthma *sounds* like it's psychosomatic. A pretty nineteen-year-old girl with a bottle of vodka in her dresser isn't a happy child. You know what I would do, Tommy, if I were you?"

"No," I said. "What would you do, Ma?"

"I would marry her. And if she doesn't make you happy, and she still has asthma and drinks a lot a year from now, I'd divorce her."

"Jesus Christ," said my sister.

"Look," said my mother. "Life works in strange ways. Take your father. When he was going to college, he worked summers at a resort in Maine. He was a waiter. The last summer he worked at that resort he met a girl named Kelly Richards. She was a guest at the hotel. Kelly was very social, very pretty, and very rich. And she was a real mover. She drank and carried on like nobody's business. She was an only daughter and she was spoiled rotten. She drove men crazy, but she fell head over heels in love with your father and would have married him in a minute. But your father dropped her and married me.

"Once I asked your father why he didn't marry Kelly Richards. He told me that playgirls like Kelly Richards were all right to fool around with at summer resorts, but not to marry. You marry nice, clean-cut, wholesome girls, he said, and that's what he did. He married nice, clean-cut, wholesome me."

My mother sighed.

"I'm sure if your father married Kelly he would have gone right into the family business—they're in publishing—and he would have lived the rich life. He wouldn't have had smelly hands from playing with people's feet all day, day after day, year after year, so he could support a wife and two kids. He wouldn't have had a stroke from worrying about how to make ends meet, and he wouldn't be on the verge of dying penniless because he wanted to send his kids through college.

"Marriage is a crap game, kids. Sometimes you have to take your chances. There are no rules. Childhood sweethearts get divorced and ex-prostitutes can make the best wives. Maybe your father should have taken a chance. He might have been fit as a fiddle and on his way to the Richards' summer home in the Bahamas today instead of sitting paralyzed in a rocking chair at Eighty-third and Broadway looking out of a window."

"Shoulda, woulda, coulda," said my sister.

Sammy met me at the train station in her shiny red Chevrolet Corvette convertible. She leaned over and opened the door on the passenger side. I walked around to the driver's side.

"Move over," I said.

"Nobody drives this car but me," said Samantha Jane Wilkerson.

27

"Either I drive," I said, "or I take the next train back to New York."

I drove.

We went to the Wilkersons' farm at Round Hill. It was where the Wilkersons kept some of their better horses, two or three cows, a well-stocked bar, and four in help.

"Can you ride?" asked Sammy.

"Horses?"

"Yes, horses."

"Sure," I said.

My horse was named Herman. When nobody was looking, I climbed up on him, put my feet in the stirrups, and said giddy-up. Herman started out of the barn, but the barn door wasn't opened all the way. The opening was *just* wide enough for Herman's body, but not for my knees and legs. Herman went out and I stayed in. I simply slid—saddle and all—down Herman's back and fell over his tail. My fall knocked the wind out of me.

We decided not to go horseback riding. We went to the Round Hill Inn instead and drank all day.

We sat at a table that overlooked a long stretch of unbelievably beautiful Connecticut countryside. It was late afternoon, and we watched the sun set. Eventually the waiter had to light the candle on our table so that we could read the dinner menu.

When we finished eating, I asked Sammy what she would like to do.

"Drive," she answered.

We drove for hours.

Sammy was drunk. She slid down deep into her seat and started talking. "I spent the first ten years of my life with a governess," she said. "I never saw my father or my mother. They were either just going somewhere or just coming back. I didn't know how lucky I was that they *weren't* around. When I got to go along, I was more miserable than before. I was constantly pushed off to my room, or entertained by a private circus, or pulled around by the chauffeur on my very own pony. My parents always seemed annoyed when I came near them. I felt that I wasn't wanted. I was a responsibility, and they didn't like responsibilities.

"My brother never paid any attention to me, either. He was too busy trying to impress his friends with all his beautiful possessions. He was the first kid on the block with everything. He *still* is.

"It never got any better. The older I got, the worse it got. I was the only child in my neighborhood that went to school in a chauffeur-driven Rolls-Royce. Do you know how embarrassing it is to go to school in a chauffeur-driven Rolls-Royce? Wow. And the Rolls-Royce was there to pick me up when school let out. And if I wanted to walk home with some friends, the Rolls-Royce would trail behind me like some big black animal. God, I hated that car.

"Sometimes my father would show a glimmer of affection. But just when I would get my hopes up, he would have to go away for some board of directors meeting, or a business convention, or a sales trip, or a stockholders meeting, or some such thing. He would call from the office and apologize. 'I'm going to be a little late tonight, bunny rabbit,' he would say, or, 'Something's come up.' *That* was it. Something's come up. He would always say, 'Something's come up.'

"Once—I was seven or eight at the time—I was sick in bed and my father promised me he would come home and play this game with me. It was a box game, I forget which one, but it was my favorite game, and I was so excited he was coming home to play it with me. I remember setting the game up, putting all the players on their squares, and getting the dice out, and the cards. And then he called. He said, 'Something's come up.' I put all the pieces back in the box and cried.

"Nothing's changed. They still don't care if I'm around. And when I *am* around, they do nothing but complain. Father's always complaining that I should be more considerate to him and Mother, and that I should be more willing to go to all their hideous social functions. And Mother's always bitching about my nails, or my hair, or my dress. My nails are too long, or my hair is too short, or my dress is not right, or it's out of style, or something. One of these days I swear I'm going to look my mother right in the eyes and tell her to go to hell."

We stopped at a tavern because Sammy wanted another drink. The place was small and smoky. On one side of the room were a couple of miniature bowling machines that you paid a quarter to play. A bunch of townies monopolized the bar, and eyed us suspiciously when we walked in. We sat at a small table in the corner. I ordered a vodka on the rocks for Sammy, and a draft beer for myself.

"I love your family," said Sammy. "They're real. It's so nice to see a real family with real problems and real happinesses. I'm so tired of the things my family thinks are problems. A new cook, a new butler, the brakes on the Rolls-Royce. Do you know what my father was complaining about yesterday? He was complaining about the shortage of qualified and trustworthy yacht captains! My father just can't find a good captain for his yacht. *That* is the biggest problem on his mind this week. Can you imagine? What a problem. And my mother. My poor, poor mother's in shock. She found my bottle of vodka."

I ordered another drink for Sammy. Her conversation depressed me and it was getting late, so I called for the check. Sammy put her drink under her jacket and we left the tavern. I headed for my sister's house in Westport. Sammy slouched down in her seat and began drinking her stolen vodka on the rocks.

"See what a lousy catch I am," she said. "I'm fat—"

"You're not fat," I said.

"And I have asthma, and all sorts of nervous twitches—"

"You only have one twitch," I said.

"And I drink too much. And I can't cook or sew. And I don't get along with one single member of my family. I don't have one redeeming quality. All I want to do is just love somebody to

30

death. I just want to get out of that rotten house and love some-body to death. All I want is someone who *needs* me and *loves* me. That's all I want. That's not asking too much, is it?"

"No," I answered feebly.

And then she cried.

"And then she cried," I told Geraldine the next morning. "She cried and cried. She was sobbing. It was as though she had this cry in her system for months and it finally came out."

"Poor kid," said my sister. We were sitting in Geraldine's kitchen having toast and coffee. It was seven o'clock. H.T. and the baby were still sleeping.

"Then she vomited," I said. "She asked me to pull the car over, and she got out and threw up. I was so embarrassed, I didn't know what to do. She was embarrassed, too. It was terrible."

My sister just kept shaking her head from side to side.

"So then I came here," I said, "and Sammy drove her car back to her house. I was afraid to let her drive, but there wasn't any-thing I could do about it. What a rotten night."

"I can imagine," Geraldine said. "How do you feel now?" She poured me another cup of coffee.

"I feel okay, I guess. Actually, what I *really* feel is scared."

"Scared?"

"Yes, scared. Sammy and I just might end up getting married, and that scares me."

"Why does that scare you?"

"Because the girl's a walking affliction, and it's not easy to fall head over heels in love with a basket case. That's what scares me."

"Bullshit," said Geraldine. "If you don't love her, you don't marry her. It's as simple as that. Mom, bless her heart, is full of crap. You don't get married with the idea that you'll get a divorce if it doesn't work in a year. What kind of shit is that?"

The next day Sammy called and said that she wouldn't blame me if I never wanted to see her again.

"I'm sorry, Tommy, I really am," she said. "I feel very ashamed of myself."

"Don't be silly. It was just one of those things."

"Do you still love me?" asked Samantha Jane Wilkerson.

"Are you kidding? Of course I do."

I wondered if she could tell I was lying.

"How can you ask a girl to marry you that you don't love?" I asked my two best friends in the world.

"It isn't easy," said Gil Mack, the twenty-eight-year-old black-sheep son of a rich candy manufacturer. Gil had never worked a day in his life. "But I'd try."

"Why?" I asked.

"Because Sammy's a nice person," answered Gil.

"You're goddamn right she is," bellowed Mike Malloy, a fat, thirty-two-year-old, red-faced Irishman, who loved his wife and four kids, and liquor, and brawls, and girls, and life, and God knows what else. "Gil's right. Sammy's a beautiful person. Better than you deserve. Forget about her money. I'm serious. She could be poor as a church mouse and it wouldn't matter. She's a beautiful person."

"She's warm and honest," said Gil.

"You're goddamn right she is," said Mike Malloy threateningly. "She's a doll. She's too good for you, you bastard. Let's have another round."

We were sitting at the bar in Mimi's restaurant. It was Friday night. Jack-the-Piano-Player was playing the piano, and my friends and I were getting drunk out of our ears. Gil Mack and Mike Malloy were crazy when they were sober. When they were drunk they were impossible.

"I need help," I said sadly.

"Hold it, Tommy," ordered Mike Malloy. "What I'm talking about is much more important."

32

Mike was talking about robbing Middletown, New Jersey.

"No kidding, it would work," said Malloy, a graduate of Cornell University and a respectable banking executive, who lived in Middletown, New Jersey. "The place is absolutely ripe for a two-million-dollar holdup. It's a wealthy community with most of its loot concentrated in a small area." He pushed aside our drinks and began sketching Middletown on a paper napkin. "Ninety percent of the town's money is in two banks and two supermarkets, all in a two-block radius."

"The hell with robbing Middletown," I said. "What do I do about Sammy?"

"Hold it! Just hear me out!" hollered Malloy, knocking over a drink with his fat arm.

"Okay, keep it down, Mike, for Christ sake!" said Mimi, scowling.

"Who am I bothering, Mimi? We're the only three people in the place."

"You're bothering *me,*" said Mimi. "I'm trying to listen to Jack, and all I hear is you."

"Mimi," I said, "tell me what I should do about Sammy."

"How the hell do I know what you should do about Sammy? Ask your friends. What are friends for?"

"I've been trying to," I moaned.

"I still think my idea's better," said Gil, "and more commercial, and safer. If we do a really good, quality pornographic movie, like the one I told you about, it would knock the country on its ass."

"Jesus Christ almighty!" I shouted.

"What?" said Jack-the-Piano-Player, his hands frozen in midair.

"I don't know what to do about Sammy," I said. *"Will somebody please tell me what the hell to do about Sammy!"*

Sammy, Gil, Mike, and myself were jammed in Gil's Morgan convertible on our way to Middletown, New Jersey. It was the first time I had seen Sammy in almost ten days.

"This is absolutely crazy," I said.

"It is not," said Malloy. "You'll see."

"It's an interesting way to spend a Saturday," said Gil.

"Listen," said Malloy. "If we *don't* rob the town, at least we'll be able to write one hell of a movie script and sell it for a fortune to Metro-Goldwyn-Mayer. Besides, Tommy, you vowed that at least I'd get a chance to show you the place."

"When did I vow that?" I asked.

"Last Friday night when the three of us were at Mimi's."

"I did? I don't remember that at all," I said.

"I'll bet that's not the only thing you don't remember," said Sammy.

"Exactly what do you mean by that?" I said indignantly.

"You proposed to me that night."

"I *what!*"

"You asked for my hand in marriage. You called me on the telephone and proposed."

"I did?"

"Yes, you did," said Sammy. "Do you remember proposing to me at all?"

"No."

"Goddamn coward had to get drunk to get the courage up to ask you to marry him, and now he doesn't even remember," growled Mike Malloy under his breath.

"What did I say?" I asked. "Was I a gentleman at least?"

"Yes," said Sammy, "you were a gentleman. This is precisely how the conversation went:

"You said, 'Sammy, let's get married.'

"I said, 'Where are you?'

"You said, 'I'm calling from a pay phone at Mimi's restaurant.' Then you said, 'Sammy, I'm serious. Let's get married.'

"I said, 'When?'

"You said, 'Soon.'

"I said, 'How soon?'

"You said, 'As soon as possible.'

"I said, 'Are you sure?'

"At that point the operator told you that your three minutes were up and to signal when you were finished.

"Then you said, 'Sammy, come on. Say yes.'

"And I said, 'Yes.'

"And you hollered, *'Great!'*

"And then I think you passed out."

"He did," said Gil, giggling. "We found him sound asleep in the phone booth."

"You said *yes?*" I asked.

"Yes, you old fart, I said yes!"

Toward the end of September I decided to take stock of myself. In doing so, I realized that I had just spent one of the most disastrous summers of my life. I had quit working at the Double-day bookstore so that I could devote all of my time to writing the Great American Novel, the first forty pages of the Great American Novel were horrendous, my unemployment was running out, and I had successfully wooed and won the hand in marriage of a girl I didn't love.

What are you going to do about all of this? I asked myself.

Nothing, I answered myself.

And so September became October.

In October Sammy dropped out of Barnard and spent her days fixing up my crummy walk-up.

"But he lives in a shithouse," my sister told Sammy.

"I know," said Sammy, "but look at all the things I can do with it."

"It's not worth it," said Geraldine.

"Yes it is."

"Why?" said Geraldine.

"Because someday I'm going to live in it, too," answered

Sammy. "Besides, Geraldine, I've always wanted to live in a candy-covered gingerbread house."

"*This* is your idea of a candy-covered gingerbread house?"

"Absolutely. All it takes is a couple of gingham curtains and Tommy."

"Hear hear," I yelled from the bathroom.

"Ridiculous," snarled Geraldine.

"What's ridiculous?" asked Sammy.

"It's just ridiculous to equate a gingerbread house with a couple of crates as end tables, some gingham curtains, and an unwashed and unemployed ne'er-do-well boyfriend, all jammed into the fifth-floor walk-up of a dilapidated East Side tenement."

"Geraldine, I think you're jealous," said Sammy.

"Samantha, I think *you're* sick. I mean, if you think washing dishes, cleaning floors, and stepping over puddles of urine in your vestibule is living, then you're out of your goddamn mind."

"I love washing dishes and cleaning floors," said Sammy, hanging up her apron, "as long as they're my dishes and my floors. Don't you know, Geraldine, that rich girls make better wives than poor girls?"

"H.T. will vouch for that," I shouted from the bathroom.

"It's true," said Sammy. "By the time a rich girl marries, she's had all the so-called better things in life. Rich girls aren't demanding. All a rich girl needs is gobs of hugs and kisses, and she's happy."

"Ridiculous," repeated Geraldine, grabbing her coat and heading for the door. Before she left, she turned to Samantha and said, "Sammy, better you than me."

Slowly but surely Sammy turned my rattrap into one of the coziest little apartments in New York. The wobbly orange crate end tables disappeared, and respectable polished pieces of furniture took their places. Lamps popped up here and there, and so did curtains, a small four-poster bed, and a bedspread.

"Where are you getting all this furniture?" I asked Sammy.

"Don't worry about it."

"I'm worrying about it."

"They'll never miss the stuff," said Sammy. "The mansion's too big. They'll just never miss it."

"Jesus Christ, Sammy," I said angrily, but way down deep I thought it was sort of great.

"You!" shouted my sister on the telephone. *"You* are the *talk* of Connecticut. I'm so proud of you I can't stand it."

"What are they talking about?" I asked.

"What are they *talking* about? They're talking about how Sammy Wilkerson dumped *the* George Larkspur, Jr., for some half-assed writer who lives in abject squalor in a roach-infested East Side tenement."

"And you're proud of *that!"* I said.

I went out and got a job.

I answered a want ad and became a part-time traveling salesman for the Transamerica Cuing Machine Company. I sold mechanical cuing devices that were used mainly on television cameras. My territory was New York, Pennsylvania, New Jersey, and Delaware. I would spend four or five days a month on the road trying to sell the cuing machines to TV stations that either had Transamerica cuing machines already or had invented something just like them themselves. Most of the time I stayed in the New York office answering service complaints on the telephone.

The only good thing about the job was that I was on an expense account when I traveled, and I didn't have to touch my salary. I wasn't making a hell of a lot, but I wasn't spending it, either.

"You're going to be the *best* salesman in the history of the Transamerica Cuing Machine Company," said Sammy proudly.

Yippee, I said to myself.

It was football season, which gave us something to do on weekends.

"Collegiate, collegiate, yes, we are collegiate," sang Gil Mack, who had been expelled from Yale in the middle of his sophomore year. Sammy and I and Mike Malloy were jammed in Gil's Morgan again. We were driving to Princeton to see the Princeton-Rutgers football game. None of us had gone to either school. It was just a good excuse to get fresh air and drunk at the same time.

In the middle of the third quarter, with Princeton about to score from the two, Sammy told me that, for some reason or other, the entire Wilkerson clan was gathering at the mansion the following Sunday. Sammy said her father had told her it was important that the two of us be there.

"Why?" I asked.

"Damned if I know. But I thought it would be a good time for you to tell my parents that we're getting married."

I immediately lost interest in the football game. For the next seven days the only thing I could think about was that coming Sunday at the Wilkersons'.

It was a cold, bleak day.

The Wilkerson family began arriving about three o'clock, and it was close to four when the last car drove up to the house. Everybody was standing or sitting in the study. I stood in a corner next to Sammy.

"Have you figured out what it's all about yet?" I whispered in Sammy's ear.

"Nope," she whispered back.

"If everyone's here, then I shall begin," said Mr. John T. Wilkerson, president and chairman of the board of the American Steel Corporation (number forty-three in *Fortune* magazine's richest one hundred companies in the United States). With that, he turned, pointed his finger at me, and said, "*You* are an opportunist! You want to marry Samantha for her money!"

I suddenly felt terribly ill.

All I could do was stand there with my hands in my pockets and stare at Mr. Wilkerson.

"Well, Christian, do you have anything to say?" asked Mr. Wilkerson.

I wasn't listening. I was noticing the hasty shift in the room toward Mr. Wilkerson and away from me. In an instant it had become Tommy Christian versus all the important members of one of the wealthiest families in America. Only Sammy's grandfather was missing on their side. He was Charles Wilkerson, the ninety-two-year-old patriarch who had migrated from Austria, or somewhere, to parlay a horse and buggy and some scrap iron into the ninth largest steel company in the world. Old man Wilkerson had gas that afternoon and was upstairs napping.

"Well, Christian," said Mr. Wilkerson impatiently, "do you or don't you have anything to say for yourself?"

No, I had nothing to say.

"Of course you don't have anything to say," said Mr. Wilkerson smugly.

I could feel this immense gloat pour across the room, filling every corner of that Victorian study. Everyone was glaring, all mouths were turned down. Even Sammy stood tight-lipped, her arms hooked behind her back, her eyes glued to the floor.

"You're pitiful, Mr. Christian," said Sammy's father. "You're someone to be pitied. You're not even clever. You're stupid. If you had a modicum of intelligence, or at least showed some cunning, I might have admired the attempt. But you are *not* intelligent. You are *not* cunning. You are just plain stupid.

"And I must say, Samantha," said Mr. Wilkerson, clearing some phlegm from his throat, "that you showed a rather small amount of intelligence yourself, to be taken in by his antics. And don't think for a minute that you fooled us. We know that you've been going to New York *not* for the shopping trips you claimed you were going for. Not at all. You were seeing *him.* We all know you enjoy playing the part of the family rebel, Samantha, but marriage is *not* a game."

Mr. Wilkerson turned toward me again but continued to talk to his daughter. "We also know, Samantha—I believe you told your brother and your brother told us—that this man had the unmitigated gall, *and* stupidity, to propose on his very first date with you! It seems that was directly after he was fired from his job as a maintenance man at some sort of bookstore."

"I was not fired, and I wasn't a maintenance man," I said in a grotesquely thin and shaky voice, barely audible to myself.

"The *only* possible thing that this man could have known about you at *that* time," said Mr. Wilkerson to Samantha, "was that you are *rich*. Isn't that right, Christian?"

"I've known your daughter since she was fourteen years old," I said.

"Oh, come on now," chided Sammy's father. I heard guffaws from other members of the family.

Mr. Wilkerson's patronizing smile quickly disappeared. His eyes turned to slits and bore down on me, but he still talked to Sammy.

"Did you know, Samantha, that the man you run so hurriedly to see in New York has been cavorting with all sorts of girls behind your back? That's quite an honorable characteristic, isn't it, Samantha? Dating girls when you're not around, and professing his love for you when you are."

"That's not true," I said.

"It is so!" shrieked Mrs. Wilkerson. *"It is absolutely so!* One of Ted's friends saw you with a girl in New York the day before Samantha was supposed to see you!"

As she spoke, Samantha's mother walked across the room until we were standing nose to nose. Her eyes, her voice, her entire being reeked of hate. She was ugly and thin and evil, and she didn't talk, she screeched.

"We know about you. We know *all* about you," hissed Mrs. Wilkerson. "You want to marry Samantha for her money, don't you? Well, you're not going to have the opportunity. We don't ever want to see you around here again, do you understand? *Never again!"*

Mr. Wilkerson cleared some more phlegm from his throat and said to his wife, "Please, Margaret. Let me handle this." He walked over and took her by the arm.

"Mrs. Wilkerson's right," he said. "We never want to see you in this house again. Do you understand? You are *never* to see Samantha again. *Never!* And, Samantha, if you try to see him, you will be dealt with severely. Furthermore, Christian, if you continue to make any attempts to see my daughter, you'll be dreadfully sorry you did, I assure you. I assume you understand me fully, Mr. Christian."

Yes, I understood. I was being banished, excommunicated, kicked out on my ass. Just a rotten chiropodist's kid out of his league and having his goddamn knuckles rapped for even thinking he could play in the big time. If I only had just a little bit of nerve, if I had any kind of guts, I'd say, Yes, Mr. Wilkerson, you can assume that I understand you fully. And while you're at it, you can make a few more assumptions.

Let's assume, I would say, that I really love your daughter. Of course, it isn't a safe assumption on my part because you wouldn't know anything about real love between a husband and wife, would you, Mr. Wilkerson? And let's assume I had absolutely no desire whatsoever to work for the American Steel Corporation. Let's just assume that I find my own way, and buy my own house, and fill it with respect and consideration instead of just priceless antiques and horse-racing ribbons. And let's assume that the manners your daughter and I would show each other would be manners based on friendship and understanding, not the hypocritical and hateful manners you show each other in this dried-up, desiccated old barn that you call home. What would you know about real manners, and real love, and real respect, and real warmth, and real consideration, Mr. Wilkerson?

And let's assume that I succeed in business on my own—not, like all the Wilkerson men, wallowing in nepotism and big fat inheritances. Let's say I make it all by myself, so that if I want to visit you on a Sunday I do because I want to, not because I *have* to. Let's just assume all that happens. Would you be able to cope with that, Mr. Wilkerson? Would you be able to digest a free spirit? Could you *understand* any of that, Mr. Wilkerson?

Would the sweetness of my love for your daughter be lost somewhere among your more serious problems, like getting a good captain for your goddamn yacht? Will the sensitivity of my caring for your alcoholic and spastic Samantha Jane be buried in your next batch of stockholders' problems? Will the gentleness of my caring for your daughter for the rest of her life screw up your last will and testament? Will you be horrified to see your daughter happy because she's with someone who loves life and loves to live instead of some goddamn socialite puppet who can't get his nose out of the *Wall Street Journal?* Will all that misunderstanding give you gas, or cause your gout to flare up?

I understand you fully, Mr. Wilkerson. I realize that you can't recognize love and warmth and tenderness and things like that because there's not one ounce of any of that in your crusty cold vapid bones. You just saved my life, Mr. Wilkerson. I could have been part of this miserable collection of people, but you wouldn't allow it, and I can't thank you enough.

And tell your beloved daughter that it's easy to take over poverty as a life style when you've had money all your goddamn life. Poverty belongs to the poor, and tell her not to forget that. And also tell your beloved daughter that when you crucify her next suitor, it might be nice if she says a word or two in his behalf, just to let the poor guy know that she's alive.

That's what I *could* have said. Weeks and months later I would tell myself I *should* have said things like that. Shoulda, woulda, coulda.

"Well, Mr. Christian, do you or don't you understand me fully?"

I didn't say anything. I just left the house.

Sammy and I walked to a little park near the Wilkerson mansion and sat on a hard green bench. It was cold and windy, and autumn leaves were swirling at our feet.

We looked everywhere but at each other. I was mortified and Sammy was a pile of utter dejection. She sat all hunched up, using one hand to keep her coat collar together. Her eye twitched continuously. I learned that it twitched more than usual when she was upset.

And then Sammy had an asthma attack.

Sammy's asthma attacks drove me out of my mind. The only thing I could do was stand there and watch a horribly predictable procedure.

First Sammy would begin to gasp for breath. Then she would fumble in her purse for her atomizer, and I would become rigid with tension until she found it. I'd watch her jam the atomizer down her throat and pump like hell, and I'd hold my breath until her face would soften and her color would return, which were the first signs that Sammy was breathing again.

Only this time Sammy's face didn't soften.

It stayed frozen and taut. Sammy couldn't breathe. No matter how hard she pumped her atomizer, she couldn't breathe. She just sat there wondering where her lungs were. You could see the fear turn to sweat all over her face. It was thirty-two degrees in that park, and she was sweating. I became incensed with the helplessness of it all.

"Christ almighty, Sammy, breathe! *Breathe! Breathe, goddamn it!*"

I jumped up, grabbed the atomizer, and started pumping it myself. And then her throat opened up, and her face softened. I stood there exhausted, staring at her. We were both panting.

Sammy drove me to the station. Before I got on the train, I turned to her and mumbled good-bye, and then added quickly, "I didn't do all those things. I really didn't."

Sammy squinched up a smile as best she could and said,

"Good-bye, Thomas," and then she walked away with her head down, and I think I heard her say, "Christ, could I use a drink."

Like I said before, looking out of train windows makes me think about things. I guess that's not unusual. So I sat there on the old New Haven Railroad and thought about things.

There I was standing in the Wilkerson study all over again, looking at Mr. John T. Wilkerson's long pointed finger and hearing him say, "*You* are an opportunist!" And hearing the witch, Mrs. Wilkerson, screech, "You want to marry Samantha for her money!" And knowing all the rest of the family were looking at me as though I was some crazy fool to think that I might ever contemplate marrying into their holy see.

The whole thing's old shoe for the Wilkersons, I thought to myself. Poor guys trying to marry heiresses wasn't anything new. Yet there was just enough pleasure in trapping the dirty opportunist to warrant an hour—not much more, though—of a Sunday afternoon, particularly in the off-season, when the tracks were closed and the Wilkerson thoroughbreds weren't running.

Bastards.

And all that stuff about asking her to marry me on our very first date. And that crap about dating girls behind Samantha's back.

Goddamnit.

As if Samantha Jane Wilkerson was such a great catch. Sure she had millions. But some poor guy was going to have to live with that eye, and those asthma attacks, and that bottle of vodka. If somebody was going to marry Samantha Jane Wilkerson for her money, he was going to have to earn every penny of it. So I'm an opportunist, am I? They should have paid *me* to take her off their hands.

When I got home, a drunken derelict was shouting messages from the gospel under my apartment window. The loud-mouth bum should be committed to an institution of some kind before he takes a leak in my foyer, I said to myself. I guess that's going to be my life. Third Avenue walk-ups that drunks can't wait to piss on.

I couldn't sleep. About four-thirty in the morning I gave up trying, and staggered into the kitchenette for a cup of coffee.

Opportunist. Of course I am, but how the hell did *they* find out?

I threw the Yuban coffee jar against the wall so hard some of the flying glass cut my face.

"How did you get those cuts on your face?" asked my sister Geraldine.

"I threw a Yuban coffee jar at my wall."

"You dumbass," snarled my sister.

"Sticks and stones may break my bones . . ."

"A lot of good throwing Yuban coffee jars around is going to do you."

I agreed.

We were sitting in a booth in the back room of P. J. Clarke's Bar & Grill.

"You mean to tell me," said Geraldine, "that you were actually going to marry Sammy for her *money?*"

"Yes."

"You don't love her at all?"

"Not really."

"And you don't feel badly about wanting to marry her for her money?"

"No."

"How can someone *do* something like that?" asked Geraldine.

"How?" I said. "I'll tell you how. Maybe it's because our mother drummed the thought to marry for money into our heads, year in and year out, from the day we were born. Or maybe it's because I'm too stupid to understand what I'm doing, or too selfish to care. I don't know.

"Maybe it's because life beats you so black and blue that you realize at an early age your mother was right: money *is* the only

45

common denominator that everybody respects, money *is* the only key to every door, and if you've got a crack at getting your hands on the stuff, grab it!

"Maybe you marry someone for their money because everything else has failed, and you don't feel like working as a damn clerk in a Doubleday bookstore forever, or living in roach-infested walk-ups for the rest of your life, or being ashamed and introverted in front of what few friends you have left because you haven't made anything out of your life and they have. Maybe you marry someone for their money because you're tired of sweating out your monthly phone bill, or being scared to get sick. But then you wouldn't know, Geraldine. You've been rich since you were seventeen years old."

"Very eloquent," said Geraldine, "but I *still* think you're a shithead, and I think you should feel terrible about this whole goddamn mess you created."

"I do feel terrible," I said, and I did. I felt terrible not because I lost the girl I loved, but because I lost millions of dollars.

Good-bye to my daydreams of writing novels on the French Riviera, or in some Swiss chalet, like some writers I heard about. Good-bye to the shiny red Corvette convertible I was just getting accustomed to driving. Good-bye security; hello phone bills, rent bills, cleaning bills, electric bills, gas bills.

"You mean you've been conning Sammy all along, just to get her inheritance?" repeated my sister, numb with shock.

"Yes."

"I can't believe this whole thing," said Geraldine. She seemed very angry. "I unknowingly introduce a con artist to one of my best friends, he screws up his con, then has the goddamn nerve to ask me for advice. Jesus, Mother, Mary and Joseph."

"Aw, come on, Geraldine," I said.

"Aw, come on, my ass," she replied, swilling down the rest of her Schlitz and wiping her mouth with her arm.

"You know, you're not to be believed, either, Geraldine," I

46

said, getting angry. "Honor society in high school, accepted at Bryn Mawr, petite, pretty, great figure, good manners, yet you curse like a truckdriver and drink beer like a longshoreman."

"Oh, shut up," she said. "Tommy, *you* are vile. You are a vile person." And then she sighed. "All right, all right." She held up her hands as if she were quieting down a thundering ovation. "Just let me ask you a question or two."

She asked seven, to be exact.

"Did Sammy say anything while her father was handing you your head?"

"No."

"You mean she didn't say a word? She didn't stick up for you, or defend you, or anything like that?"

"No."

"Why not?"

"I don't know."

"Do you think Sammy loved you *before* her father accused you of being an opportunist?"

"Yes."

"By some crazy miracle," continued Geraldine, "do you think she *still* might love you now?"

"I don't know," I said, feeling a strange pang somewhere in my body.

"Are you really—I mean *were* you really chasing Sammy just for her money? Now answer me honestly."

"In all honesty, yes. I wouldn't admit that to anybody else in the world, Geraldine, but if she wasn't an heiress, I wouldn't take her to a movie."

"I can't believe you, Tommy. I really can't believe you. How *could* you be so coarse? How could you be such a goddamned sniveling runt to go after one of my closest friends for her *money!* You know something, Tommy? You're a craphead."

Geraldine stared at her lap and shook her head back and forth several times. She finally looked up with a very nasty expression

47

on her face and said, "Tommy, you're a real bastard. But you *are* my brother and I *do* love you. I guess blood *is* thicker than water. It must be, because I'm going to tell you how you can *still* marry Sammy."

"You're kidding!" I said. "How?"

"Sammy's a rebel, right?"

"Right."

"Okay," said my sister, moving closer to the table. "If she loves you, I mean *really* loves you, she won't let *anybody* in her family push her around. She never has."

"So?"

"So call her up and ask her two things. First ask her why she didn't defend you or tell her father to go to hell when he was cremating you. She should have stuck up for you instead of standing there like a mute. If you think her answer makes sense, then ask Sammy the second question."

"Which is?"

"Ask her if she will live with you. Tell her to pack her bags and move into your crusty gingerbread thing she supposedly loves so much."

"Jesus," I replied.

"If she does, Tommy, she'll put her family, and the entire iron and steel industry, in a catatonic state."

"What's that?"

"A catatonic state? It's a schizophrenic disorder characterized by a plastic immobility of the limbs. It's a favorite expression of mine."

Silence.

"Geraldine."

"What?"

"You're not serious?"

"Of course I am. Listen, if she leaves Greenwich and moves into your crummy shithouse, I guarantee you her father will do one of two things: he'll either arrange to have your apartment dynamited or drag the two of you to the nearest altar. And they won't disinherit her, either, simply because they can't! Sammy once told me that legally she *had* to get I don't know how many millions of dollars because that's just the way it is."

"*When* does she get the millions?" I asked anxiously. "Did she tell you *when* she gets them?"

"When she's twenty-one."

My sister then screamed, *"Waiter, can we have the goddamned check, please!"* In a flash, she sucked in the remnants of the beer foam in her glass, grabbed her coat, scarf, and purse, and slid out of the booth. "I've got to catch a train," she said.

Before she disappeared, she turned and hollered, *"Hey, Tommy, if it works you're going to owe me one hell of a goddamned favor, you bastard!"* Everyone in the bar looked at her, then at me.

Living in New York has its compensations. If you want to walk around and think about things, there are lots of places to do it. Some of my favorite thinking places were the zoo, the courtyard of the Museum of Modern Art, the water fountain next to the Corning Glass building, the ice skating rink in Central Park, and Saint Patrick's Cathedral.

I always sat in the back row of Saint Fat's. I felt self-conscious sitting up front. I kept imagining that all the worshipers sitting behind me knew I wasn't Catholic and that I was just there for some selfish personal reason like trying to decide whether I should call Sammy and ask her to live with me.

Wow.

To challenge the Wilkerson cartel was *some* undertaking. I sat in Saint Patrick's for six straight nights and begged for help, but nothing happened. No bolt of lightning struck me. No fantastic apparition burst forth to tell me what to do. Nothing. Maybe that's when I became an atheist.

On the night of the seventh day, I decided to call Samantha. Geraldine was probably right. Like she always says, the best defense is a good offense. I practiced my opening lines for over an hour and then I placed the call. When Samantha answered, I forgot what I was going to say.

"Sammy," I said, with all the authority I could muster up, "why haven't I heard from you?"

"Because I was afraid that you were terribly angry and that you would take your anger out on me." And then her voice dropped to just above a whisper. "Besides," she said, "I felt that if you really loved me, you would call sooner or later."

"Christ, after all that abuse I took! Jesus, Samantha, if you loved *me* you would have called days ago."

"Thomas, what the hell are you yelling about? We're talking to each other now, aren't we?"

So we were. Then I remembered what I had rehearsed saying.

"Sammy," I said, "why didn't you say something, *anything*, all the time your father was tearing me apart in your study? All I remember is you standing in the corner with your hands behind your back. Did you believe him? Was that it? Did you believe the things he was saying about me?"

"No."

"Then why didn't you say something?"

"I guess I was too stunned to say something," she replied. "I was in shock. I was mortified. I couldn't comprehend what I was seeing and hearing. I couldn't believe what was happening. I just couldn't believe it. I was numb. I think I still am."

I took a deep breath.

"Sammy," I said, "don't let your family push you around. You never have. Don't start now. The only thing they can do to you is disinherit you, and if they do, so what? It's *me* who's going to take care of us, anyway. I'm going to make it, Sammy, somehow I'm going to make it. I know it and you know it, so what are we worried about? And I'll always take care of you. It'll always be just you and me, babe. That's the way I want it to be and that's the way it *will* be. I love you, Sammy, and I promise I'll take care of you for the rest of my life."

I stopped, but started again quickly before Sammy could say anything.

"What can your family do to you, Sammy? Put you in jail? Send you to Europe? Pick you up bodily and put you on an ocean liner? I mean, what can they do to you?"

I paused. Nothing happened on the other end of the phone, so I went on.

"Sammy, the hell with them. It's about time they realized that you're grown up and that you can do what you want to do. Sammy . . ."

I gulped.

"Sammy, pack your bags and move in with me."

Nothing. Not even breathing on the other end.

"Sammy, did you hear what I said?"

"Yes," she answered.

I began to feel embarrassed.

"Well?"

Nothing again. I started to panic.

"Sammy, if I said something wrong, I apologize, but that's how I feel. Whatever I said is straight from the heart. As corny as it sounds, it's straight from the heart. Honest. Think it over, Sammy. Please."

"Okay."

"Good-bye, Sammy."

"Good-bye, Thomas."

I hung up the phone. I felt like a silly idiot.

Goddamn Geraldine. Goddamn my sister. She did that purposely. She wanted to embarrass me, that's what she wanted. She wanted me to learn a lesson by making me feel like a fool, and I listened to her. I fell for it, goddamnit, I fell for it.

Goddamn my sister.

I sat by the telephone all night waiting for Sammy's call, but she never called.

I stayed home from work the next day and waited. About four

o'clock in the afternoon the phone rang. It scared the hell out of me. I grabbed it like a shot. It wasn't Sammy. It was my goddamn sister.

"Did you call her?" she asked.

"Yes, I called her."

"So?"

"So you and your goddamn ideas. And me!" I shrieked. "I've got to be the world's biggest jerk. I listened to you!"

"What the hell are you talking about? For Christ sake, Tommy, this phone call is costing me a fortune and you're screwing around with riddles. What the hell happened?"

I was so mad it hurt.

"You know something, Geraldine? You *do* curse too much for a goddamn girl." I hung up on her.

I went for a walk. It was one of the coldest Decembers in the history of New York but I went for a walk. I walked for hours.

When I got back to my place, Sammy was there.

Strange things happen when you're living with someone you're trying to impress. Basic everyday habits take on bewilderingly illogical proportions, and life's emphasis begins to appear in uncustomary places, like going to the bathroom, the way your hair looks in the morning, the clothes you wear, and what a frighteningly habitual animal you really are.

The girls I used to live with, the transients who drifted in and out like the tides, didn't mean a thing to me, so going to the bathroom was an unimportant event. I just went to the bathroom. But after Sammy moved in, I began shutting the door, running the faucet, and flushing *before* I was finished. I also sprayed tons of Glade mist about, which in most cases was totally uncalled for.

And my hair.

I suddenly became aware of my hair, particularly in the morning when I woke up and it looked exactly like shredded wheat. I obviously had woken up many times in the past with that shredded wheat look without getting all spastic about it. But after

Sammy moved in, the look bothered me. In fact, it bothered me so much that I would sneak out of bed in the morning before Sammy opened her eyes, so that I could take a shower and get my mop plastered down as fast as I could.

I also realized how infrequently I visited the cleaners. It became sadly apparent that I would wear certain favorite articles of clothing endlessly. It was also obvious how bad these few specific sportshirts, sweaters, and dungarees smelled.

I decided I was extremely gross.

I was also extremely fastidious, which is a rare combination.

I could never understand why Sammy wouldn't put the hairbrush back exactly where it came from on the dresser, or why she never returned the cigarette lighter to its proper coffee table. And though I didn't say anything, I was constantly annoyed that Sammy refused to wring out the washcloth and drape it over the hot water knob when she finished showering. I always did, because that's where a used washcloth belonged.

And then one day I stopped and shuddered at what a meticulously neat bore I was.

"You know, Thomas, you're a meticulously neat bore," Sammy told me three days after she arrived. "Either loosen up or get ready for a breakdown, because I'm *not* a meticulously neat bore. I haven't noticed but I'll bet you fold your pants by the creases and lay them over the back of a chair before you go to sleep. Do you do that, Thomas?"

"Aw, come on," I answered, trying to sound amazed that a thought like that would even enter her mind. The frightening thing was that I always *did* fold my pants by the creases and drop them over a chair when I took them off.

That night, before we went to bed, I kicked my pants clear across the room with such gusto that I was afraid I had overexaggerated the move.

"Well, at least he doesn't fold his pants by the creases," mumbled Sammy to herself. I never have since.

After a week things got better. I did what Sammy suggested. I loosened up.

"Can I ask you something?" Sammy said one night just before we went to sleep.

"Sure."

"How come you walk around lately with your hair all plastered down? I like it the way it is when you wake up, all fuzzy and frumpy. It looks cute. It looks like Brillo."

I smiled. Brillo. And all this time I thought my hair looked like shredded wheat.

"Can I ask you something else?"

"You can ask me a whole lot of things," I said.

"You once told me you were an atheist. Are you still?"

"I guess so," I replied.

"Didn't you say you sat in Saint Patrick's Cathedral for six nights in a row wondering whether I'd come to live with you if you asked me to?"

"Yes."

"Well, I'm here, aren't I? And you're not even Catholic. Good night, Thomas."

Sammy asked if I had spoken to my sister Geraldine lately. I hadn't.

I didn't call my sister for two reasons. One was the frantic pace of the past week, and the other—the more important reason— was that Geraldine was probably mad at me for hanging up on her, and *that* scared me.

I thanked Sammy for reminding me, and called Westport, Connecticut. Geraldine's husband answered the phone.

"Hello, H.T., this is Tommy. How are you?"

"Fine, Tommy. How are you?"

"Okay. Is my sister there?"

"Yes, she is, Tommy, but I might as well warn you. She's—"

"Miffed at me," I cut in smartly.

"I'd say something more than miffed," corrected H.T.

"More than miffed?" I repeated. "Well, don't worry, H.T. I'll just lay some of the old family charm on her and she'll melt like butter."

"I love your sister a lot, Tommy, but I've never seen her melt like butter. I'll get her."

My heart palpitated a little bit.

Geraldine picked up the phone.

"Craphead," she said sweetly.

"Hi, Geraldine."

"Don't give me that 'Hi, Geraldine' shit. You call me in a trauma and I break my hump to get down to New York to hold your hand on a freezing cold day with a pregnant stomach—"

"Pregnant!" I gasped.

". . . for a lousy glass of beer and a hamburger, which I have to gulp down so I can catch a train and get back to my husband, who can't get over the way I'm running around in the condition I'm in, and do you call me to let me know what happened? No! I have to call *you!* So I call you, and what happens? You *hang up on me!* Hey, Tommy . . ."

I knew what was coming.

"Up yours!"

Geraldine hung up on me. We were even.

Sammy and I lived together for two weeks before it dawned on me that she never said a word about her parents. Nor had her parents tried to contact her. Or had they?

"It's been weeks since you left home," I said casually over my Sunday *New York Times* sports section. "I wonder if anybody in your family knows you're missing."

"They know," said Sammy.

"They *do!*" I said, remaining behind the newspaper.

"My mother's secretary called while you were in Buffalo."

"What did she say?" I asked, trying to hide my nervousness.

"She said that my mother and father were upset."

"And . . ."

"And that I should come home immediately."

"And . . ." I noticed my heart beating.

"I asked my mother's secretary why my father and mother delegated to *her* the responsibility of calling me. If my father was so concerned, why didn't *he* phone himself? My mother's secretary said that, for one thing, he was too upset, and for another thing, he was terribly tied up with a board of directors meeting that was about to take place. And Mother had several art appreciation tours to conduct through the mansion during the past week. Can you believe that? Her daughter's run away to live with a man in New York and she can't make a phone call because she's conducting art appreciation tours.

"Anyway, I thanked my mother's secretary and asked her to deliver a message for me. I told her to tell my parents that I had no intentions of coming home. I told her to tell them that for the first time in my life I had found happiness in this beautiful apartment. I told her to tell them that nobody was hassling me or telling me how long my nails should be, or how much makeup I should wear, or what social events I had to attend. I told her to tell them that I was finally living in a place where there wasn't yelling and fighting all the time. There was kissing and hugging and loving instead. I told her to tell them that life had become peaceful for a change, and that it was nice.

"I told her to tell them that even if I caught a venereal disease from you, or if I was mugged by our next-door neighbor, I wouldn't come back to Greenwich. At least you and the neighbor would be paying some honest-to-goodness attention to me. I don't have to be a member of the board of directors or some social patron of the arts to get your attention."

"Why didn't you tell me this before?" I asked.

"You don't need the aggravation," Sammy said. She put her face in her hands. "One of these days I'm going to tell my mother to go to hell."

Then she cried.

I walked up behind her and patted the top of her head.

"Hey, Sammy, cut it out," I said. "Come on, cut it out."

I stood there patting her head like you pat a puppy dog. I didn't know what else to do. I felt so helpless. If there was anything I hated to see, it was a girl crying.

"Aw, come on, Sammy, stop crying. Please, I hate to see you cry."

After a minute or so, she looked up at me. Her face was sopping wet but she wriggled it into a smile.

The Wilkersons are real bastards, I said to myself. They shouldn't hurt her like they do. How much can the kid take?

Later that night we had dinner at Mimi's. I had called Mike Malloy and Gil Mack and asked them to join us, but neither was available. Mike was immobilized by a gigantic hangover and Gil was in the middle of a complicated plan to seduce a pale, introverted, brunette tambourine player with a local Salvation Army band. So Sammy and I ate alone, which was just as well.

"You know, Sammy, you should be very happy you asked me to marry you," I said above the din of Mimi's standard Sunday tirade with his chef.

"I asked you to *what!*"

"You could have asked one of those social butterflies you used to date," I continued, oblivious to her small interruption, "whose concept of excitement is taking a sauna bath with his father at the club. I can just see you up to your ass in PTA meetings, Art Center League gatherings, and church socials."

"There's nothing wrong with PTA meetings."

"I'm sure that George Larkspur Carruthers—"

"George Carruthers Larkspur," corrected Sammy.

". . . would insist on visiting the mansion at least twice a week to pay homage to your mother and father."

"At least twice a week."

"Sounds like a fascinating life to me."

"Sounds grisly to me," said Sammy.

"You still have time," I said, feigning thick concern. "Maybe you ought to think it over."

"Can I finish my spaghetti first?"

"It's going to be a tough haul climbing up that ladder of success," I said melodramatically. "The road to the top may be fraught with problems."

"Sounds rather grim," said Sammy, smiling.

"And I'm not so sure you have what it takes to make that haul."

"Test me."

"Of course, I'm going to succeed brilliantly."

"Of course."

"There's no doubt in my mind that I will become one of the wealthiest men in America."

"No question about it."

"Consequently, if you're marrying me for my money, you better think it over. Like my sister always says, if you marry for money, you earn it."

"Your sister has a way with words."

"So if you *are* marrying me for my money, and considering what lies ahead . . ."

"The relentless, merciless, implacable climb to the top . . ."

"Exactly. And knowing that now, as you do, there's still time for you to get out. Now's your chance to run."

"And leave our cozy apartment, after all the work I put into it?"

"I still think you should consider marrying George Carruthers Larkspur."

"Like your sister says, shoulda woulda coulda."

That night, when we went to bed, I had this absurd feeling that I might conceivably love Samantha Jane Wilkerson, one of the richest girls in America.

The next day was Monday.

That was the day Mr. Wilkerson's secretary telephoned me at work and asked if I would please meet Mr. Wilkerson at the

American Steel Building, twenty-fourth floor, at 5 P.M. He wanted to see me, alone.

I called Sammy and told her.

"Give 'im hell, you old fart," she replied.

"Send Samantha back home within twenty-four hours," said Mr. John T. Wilkerson, "and you can marry her."

I was sitting in a huge black leather chair across from Sammy's father, who was also sitting in a huge black leather chair. Mr. Wilkerson had an office that resembled a living room, not an office. There wasn't any desk. Just a lot of thick leather chairs and couches, and heavy end tables and coffee tables. There were half a dozen expensive paintings on the walls, and a quartet of silver-framed pictures on his bar. The pictures were of Mr. Wilkerson, Mrs. Wilkerson, son Ted, and daughter Samantha. They looked like your standard happy American family.

Mr. Wilkerson cleared some phlegm from his throat and continued. "You can marry Samantha right after the holidays, say the second week in January, or you can wait until we return from Scottsdale in April and get married then. If you choose to get married right after the holidays, it will be a small wedding with just the immediate family. If you wait until we come back from Arizona, we will give you a big wedding with all the trimmings. Mrs. Wilkerson and I would prefer to give Samantha a big wedding. We have a great many friends and business associates we would like to invite to our daughter's wedding, and we wouldn't have the time to prepare for *that* large an event in just four weeks. In any case, the choice is yours, *if* you send Samantha home by tomorrow."

"I will send Samantha home tomorrow," I said, "and we will get married *before* you go away."

"So be it," said Mr. Wilkerson with a sigh.

For a moment—just a split second, and for reasons I couldn't comprehend—I think I pitied the man. But then he stood, signaling me curtly that the meeting was over, and I didn't pity him at all.

I could hardly control myself, going down the elevator. I was grinning from ear to ear, and stayed that way for all twenty-four floors.

Outside, I jumped high into the air and clicked my heels, first on one side, then on the other, and let out an ear-splitting war whoop.

I was going to marry Samantha Jane Wilkerson! I had pulled it off. Tommy Christian, the poor chiropodist's son from row-house Queens, was going to marry Samantha Jane Wilkerson, daughter of one of the richest families in America.

Jesus, Mother, Mary and Joseph.

I had a most unusual Christmas.

I went from a drab existence in a drafty New York walk-up to a Connecticut social whirl I never knew existed. Dinner parties, the country club, formal dances, the whole works. The only thing that was missing was my family. They were never included, not even my sister Geraldine and H.T.

I thought about saying something to the Wilkersons, but I changed my mind. Why rock the boat?

"What's the matter?" growled my sister on the telephone. "Are we the plague? I mean, do the Wilkersons think that if they should, God forbid, brush up against a Christian, they'll get a rash? Who does Margaret Wilkerson think your mother is, Typhoid Mary?"

"Aw, come on, Geraldine."

"Don't give me your aw-come-on crap. Just remember, Tommy, you weren't placed here on earth. You came from a family."

Geraldine was absolutely right, but I didn't know what to do. Sammy did it for me.

The night after Geraldine called me to complain about the cold shoulder she and my mother were getting from the Wilkersons, I was invited to a dinner party at the Wilkerson mansion that included Sammy, Mr. and Mrs. Wilkerson, brother Ted, and Ted's latest wealthy and toothy all-American girl friend. This one was from Smith, and she played field hockey. She looked it. Her name was Regina Oxley, and though it was hard to believe, her friends actually called her Kitten. Kitten Oxley. My sister would have had a few things to say about *that!*

Anyway, it was just a simple Thursday night dinner at an end-lessly long dinner table that seemed extra long because there were just the six of us. Sammy and I sat on the same side, and if I extended my right arm sideways as far as I could and Sammy extended her left arm, they wouldn't have touched.

Mr. and Mrs. Wilkerson directed their entire conversation to brother Ted and Kitten Oxley. Sammy and I might just as well have been eating in the kitchen. They were all discussing a cock-tail party the Wilkersons were throwing that Sunday at the coun-try club in honor of *our* forthcoming marriage. The party was for business associates they considered "family." Halfway through the meal, Sammy interrupted, which came as a shock to all of us. How *dare* she speak?

"I want Tommy's mother, Geraldine, and H.T. at that party. I would want Tommy's father, but I know he wouldn't be able to come because he's so sick. But I want the rest of Tommy's family at that party."

Mr. and Mrs. Wilkerson looked at Sammy, then at each other, and finally continued talking where they had left off, as if Sam-my's sentences never were spoken.

"Did anyone hear what I just said?" asked Sammy, never taking her eyes off her plate.

"Samantha!" said Mr. Wilkerson. That's all he said, just "Samantha," only he broke it up into three distinct parts, with the accent on the middle syllable: "Sa-*man*-tha!"

Sammy didn't even look up. She calmly sliced a piece of roast beef, pushed it on her fork with her knife, and said, "If Mrs. Christian, and Geraldine, and H.T. are *not* at Sunday's party, I'll move back to Tommy's apartment on Monday, and you can forget about the wedding, and you can also forget about me moving out of his place again to accommodate you, unless of course Tommy throws me out." She put the roast beef in her mouth and chewed.

Mrs. Wilkerson threw her napkin down into her plate, which was full of food, and shot up to a standing position.

"Samantha, I will *not* have you talk to us like that, do you hear? I will *not* be threatened by you! Just *who* do you think you are? I'm almost a nervous wreck as it is from this damn wedding of yours. It's not easy planning a wedding in four weeks, particularly at this time of year, *and* with all the other social functions your father and I have to attend."

"Margaret, please," whined Mr. Wilkerson, but Sammy's mother refused to stop. She crossed her arms and continued screeching, pointing her finger at me as she screeched. "I begged your father to let you stay in New York with him for the rest of your life. I'm going to get *sick* from this, and it will be all your fault, Samantha. *It will be all your fault!*"

Mrs. Wilkerson pushed her chair back and walked off to a corner of the room. She stood there facing the wall, as if she were a dunce.

Sammy didn't flinch. Her eye was twitching up a storm, but she didn't flinch. Not outwardly.

"Please, please," said Mr. Wilkerson. "For God's sake, we have company here." I'm sure he was referring to Kitten Oxley, not me.

"Please my foot," said Sammy. "The two of you have pushed me around for nineteen years, but this is *one* time you're not going to. You've insulted me, ignored me, belittled me, and almost destroyed me. Never once has either of you *ever* showed me any respect. But I swore to myself years ago that when it came to my wedding, I would demand your respect and get it. My wedding is the most important event of my life. It means starting a new life with the man I love, and I don't intend to have either of you endanger that start. You will not insult my fiancé or my fiancé's family. Tommy's mother and sister and Harrison will be at this Sunday's party, and every other party that you give before the wedding, or the Wilkersons will have the biggest public scandal in the history of this pompous and decrepit family." Sammy helped herself to some asparagus.

Mrs. Wilkerson whirled around from her corner and glared at Sammy for a full thirty seconds, and then she left the room. Mr. Wilkerson got up and started to leave, but stopped and turned to Sammy.

"I think you owe your mother *and* myself an apology. And I think you can apologize to your brother and Miss Oxley for causing such an unfortunate scene."

Mr. Wilkerson left the room.

Ted Wilkerson and Kitten Oxley left the room.

"One of these days," said Sammy, "I'm going to tell my mother to go to hell." Then she finished her roast beef.

Four days before the wedding, Sammy and I were summoned to appear at noon on the twenty-fourth floor of the American Steel Building. "Nothing to worry about," said Mr. Wilkerson to me on the telephone, in a voice more cheerful than I had ever heard before. "Just a few little things we have to clear up before you two get married."

"What do you think it's about?" I asked Sammy, going up in the elevator.

"I don't know," she answered.

Sammy and I were ushered into Mr. Wilkerson's living room–office by his elderly, gray-haired secretary. Mr. Wilkerson was sitting in his favorite chair. Another man was sitting in the chair

I had sat in before. He was a lawyer, Mr. Wilkerson explained, and a friend of the family. The lawyer bowed his head low and smiled, as if he were taking a curtain call.

Mr. Wilkerson discussed the cold spell. We all agreed it was quite cold. The lawyer smiled again and Mr. Wilkerson got to the point.

"As you know, Samantha, you are a very wealthy girl. You have several trusts in your name that I'm quite sure you're not even aware of. For instance, you probably know that your mother and I have set up a trust for you, but did you know that your grandfather has set up a trust in your name, too?"

Samantha said she didn't know that.

Mr. Wilkerson said he didn't think she did, the lawyer smiled, I smiled, and Mr. Wilkerson continued.

"I'm also quite sure, Samantha, that you are totally unaware of the size of these trusts. Since financial affairs never seem to concern you, your mother and I saw no reason to bring these matters to your attention. Now, however, I believe the time has come for you to be apprised of your impending financial state."

Mr. Wilkerson cleared some phlegm from his throat and said, "Your grandfather's trust is worth close to five million dollars. The principal of the trust your mother and I have set up for you is now worth roughly three million dollars. The combined principal of the two trusts is therefore approximately eight million dollars, which obviously provides you with a substantial amount of income each year; somewhere in the neighborhood of a quarter of a million dollars. That comes to about five thousand dollars a week, after taxes," said Mr. Wilkerson. He smiled. So did the lawyer and so did I.

Sammy wasn't smiling, so I stopped.

"You will never be allowed to touch the principal of your grandfather's trust," said Mr. Wilkerson. "That's how your grandfather always sets up his trusts. It's no different in structure than the trusts he's established for all his children and grandchildren. Our trust, the one your mother and I have provided for you, is somewhat different. You *can* use the principal of this trust if you so desire, although if the time ever came to consider that, I would recommend highly against it. As I mentioned before, the income from the two trusts is substantial enough to live on for the rest of your life, and I can't comprehend any need so great that would necessitate your touching the principal of the trust we've set up for you. Do you follow me so far, Samantha? I'm sure that, as far as you're concerned, this is a boring subject, but I do think it's important that you understand what I am saying."

Samantha said that she understood what her father was saying and that the subject wasn't boring.

"Fine," said Mr. Wilkerson.

He stood up, cleared some more phlegm from his throat, and began strolling around his office. He talked as he strolled.

"Now, as you know, or perhaps you don't, you're not allowed to touch any of your income until you're twenty-one. Again, this is the same for all the Wilkerson trusts that have been established for the family's children. However, your twenty-first birthday is a little less than two years away."

My heart began pounding.

Something was up.

"Now, Samantha," continued Mr. Wilkerson, clearing his throat, "your mother and I have been giving a lot of thought to you and Tommy, and we've decided that the two of you certainly don't want the financial problems that go with handling such large sums of money. Of course, you could hire a financial adviser to take over the major portion of that burden, but it's still a rather awesome and time-consuming responsibility."

Mr. Wilkerson sat down.

"Also it's not healthy," he said.

"What's not healthy?" asked Samantha.

"Your mother and I decided that it's not healthy to begin married life with so much money and security at your command.

65

We're sure that you and Tommy would rather start your life together the same as any other young couple, with the same thrills and disappointments inherent in making your own way. After all, a substantial part of the excitement of being newlyweds is experiencing the bad as well as the good, don't you agree?" Samantha's father looked at both of us for an answer. Neither of us said anything.

"Consequently, Samantha," said the lawyer and friend of the family, "your father and mother and your grandfather have changed the mechanics of your trusts, in a legal manner, so that you will be prohibited from acquiring any of the principal or income of either of your trusts for an additional twenty years. In other words, you will not be able to spend one dollar of your money until nineteen eighty-three.

"Also, your grandfather has given your parents the power of attorney to control the income of the trust he set up for you. Therefore, the only way you can get *any* of the income from *either* trust sooner than nineteen eighty-three is if your mother or father stipulates you should. Your father wanted you and Mr. Christian to be aware of these facts before the wedding on Monday."

The lawyer smiled.

Mr. Wilkerson smiled.

I couldn't believe my ears. The bastards were disinheriting Sammy.

I felt sick.

Twenty years! Christ, when she finally comes into her money, I'll be forty-five years old!

"Do you have any questions, Samantha?" asked Mr. Wilkerson.

"Yes, just one," said Samantha. "Will all the Wilkerson children and grandchildren be prevented from spending their money for an additional twenty years?"

"No," said Sammy's father. "Just you."

Sammy and I went to Mimi's for lunch. I wasn't hungry at all, but I forced myself to eat so that Sammy wouldn't think I wasn't hungry at all.

Strangely enough, Sammy seemed almost happy.

"I *knew* they would," she said. "I would have been astonished if they hadn't. Anyway, I'm glad they did. Now there are no strings attached to me *or* you. They have no holds on us. *That*, in itself, is almost worth the money."

"Almost," I said. I was instantly sorry I said it.

"Don't worry, Thomas. You don't need any Wilkerson help. You're going to do it all by yourself. It'll be either a job, or your writing, or something, but you're going to do it. I know. I'm a witch. And besides, we don't have to be rich to be happy, do we?" She chucked me under the chin and smiled.

No, we don't, but it would sure help.

"As long as we have each other," continued Sammy, "we'll be just fine."

Sure we will. I'll be selling cuing devices the rest of my life so that I can afford to pay for your asthma atomizers.

"Now it will *really* be just you and me, babe," said Sammy.

Afflicted you and traveling salesman me.

I took Sammy to Grand Central Station so that she could catch the six-thirty train back to Greenwich.

"I'm going to have to stop bagging work," I said. "I can't afford to get fired now." I pushed out a miserable chuckle.

"Oh, get off it, you old fart," said Sammy. "You're not the only guy who has to work for a living." She tightened my scarf and pulled my overcoat collar closed. "Keep yourself warm. Can't get sick now. You're going to have a wife to take care of."

We kissed and Sammy got on the train. I watched through the windows until she found a seat. She took off her coat and threw it into the rack over her head. Then she walked back up the aisle to the doorway. The conductor was standing next to her when she leaned out of the door and yelled, "See you in four days, *unless* you were intending to marry me for my money."

"And what if I *was* marrying you for your money?" I hollered.

"Then now's *your* chance to run," she yelled, straining to be heard as the train disappeared down the tunnel.

And that's exactly what I did.

I ran.

That night at Mimi's, I talked Gil Mack and Mike Malloy into driving up to Martha's Vineyard for the weekend.

"It'll be great there," I said. "Martha's Vineyard is empty this time of year. Just the ocean and the sea gulls, and a few good restaurants. It's a good place to let your head air out."

"But you're getting married in three days," said Mike Malloy. It was more like an order than a statement.

"Don't you think I know that?"

"But don't you have things to do?"

"I've done everything. Besides, I need one last weekend of freedom with the two best friends I have on earth."

We left the next morning.

On the way, we stopped for beer in Groton and Mystic. We also stopped for beer at Poquonock Bridge, Pawcatuck, Westerly, Narrangansett, Newport, New Bedford, and Falmouth. We never made it to Martha's Vineyard that night. We missed the ferry.

So we stayed in Woods Hole and continued drinking in an artsy-craftsy little whaling pub near the pier.

I sat at the bar and stared at my beer. For a while I didn't hear a word Gil and Mike were saying. All I did was think about Sammy. I thought about her twitching eye, and her asthma, and about the money, and the wedding, and about my plan not to show up, and about hurting her feelings. I thought a lot about hurting her feelings.

I also thought about some of the good times we had together. Sammy and I *did* have some good times together.

At one point I overheard Sammy's name mentioned. Mike was telling Gil that Sammy was the kind of girl that makes a good wife. He was saying, "I have my own theories about love and marriage. The one thing I've learned after being married for ten years to the same woman, and watching my friends get divorced, is that the fiery romances and the passionate love affairs never work. And unfortunately, that's what everyone keeps looking for. The guy wants to see Fourth of July fireworks every time he looks into his girl's eyes, and she wants Roman candles to go off in her heart with each kiss."

"Very poetic," said Gil Mack.

"And both of them get disappointed and scared when it stops happening," continued Mike Malloy. "And it usually stops happening the day after they're married."

"That's why I say friendship is more important than passion. If your wife turns out to be your best friend, and you turn out to be *her* best friend, and you never lose your respect for each other, and you're loyal to each other in good times as well as bad—"

"Sometimes good times can be rougher than bad times," interrupted Gil.

"Right!" agreed Mike boisterously. "That's so true."

Balls, I thought. How could good times possibly be rougher than bad times?

"But as I said," continued Mike, "if you and your wife can be truly good friends to each other, *then* you have a chance for a happy marriage. *That's* the kind of marriage that works, and that's why I think Sammy is so great. She'll be the best friend Tommy ever had."

"Bravo!" yelled Gil Mack.

And that's when I told Mike and Gil I wasn't going to marry Sammy.

I told them about our meeting with Mr. Wilkerson and the lawyer, and how they disinherited her. I confessed that the only reason I wanted to marry Sammy in the first place was for her money, and now she was disinherited. I also told them about all of Sammy's problems, like her twitching eye, and her asthma, and her drinking.

"You're kidding about wanting to marry Sammy just for her money," said Gil.

"No, I'm not," I said, and I was pretty sure I wasn't. And if I wasn't, then why the hell would I want to marry a girl with all her problems if she was poor to boot?

"Why would I?" I asked, but nobody answered.

I said that I planned to stay on at Martha's Vineyard and not go back to New York on Sunday. I told them that I had my life's savings with me, all five hundred and sixty dollars, and that if I found an inexpensive room somewhere I could probably live on the island for at least a few months.

"Does Sammy know you're standing her up at the altar?" asked Mike Malloy.

"No. Anyway, it'll serve all those goddamn Wilkersons right. It'll sure take care of them."

"How's that?" asked Mike, angrier than I had ever seen him in my entire life.

"They've hated me all along. They never wanted me to marry their precious little daughter in the first place. Well, the hell with them. They can *have* their precious little daughter, and I hope Mrs. Wilkerson drops dead from the shock of me not showing up for her fucking wedding of the year."

"That sure takes good care of the Wilkersons," said Mike. "They end up not having the marriage they never wanted, Sammy doesn't get the marriage she's *always* wanted, and, according to you, that's taking care of the Wilkersons. You're shitting all over Sammy, and, according to you, that's taking care of the Wilkersons. You're so full of crap, Tommy, it's coming out of your ears."

"This whole thing doesn't really sound like something you'd do," said Gil Mack.

"It's a goddamn shitty trick, if you ask me," said Malloy.

"Nobody asked you, Mike."

"Well, I'm *telling you*. It's a goddamn shitty trick."

I thought for a moment that Mike Malloy was going to punch me in the mouth.

We took the morning ferry to the island.

I was in a sizable funk. I also had a sizable hangover. Mike was in a rotten mood, but Gil was chipper. He always was.

We found rooms at a place called the Hopkins House. Mr. Hopkins was a retired architect who had left Vermont to spend his senior years building model sailing ships and taking in boarders on the island. His wife was terribly quaint and New Englandy, just like the Hopkins House.

The three of us drove into town and walked around, window-shopping. It was freezing. All of our ears were numb, so we bought three pairs of earmuffs. Eventually we found a bar that was open and began drinking again. About an hour later, Mike asked me if I still wasn't going to show up for the wedding on Monday.

I told him that I still wasn't going to show up for the wedding on Monday.

"Then I'm going back today," he said. "I don't believe in what you're doing, so I don't want any part of it. Besides, I don't want to give aid and comfort to an asshole. I happen to like Sammy a lot."

"I guess I'll go back, too," said Gil Mack. "I love you, Tommy, but your mind's a boggle, and since my mind's always a boggle, all I can do is fuck you up even more than you are right now, if that's possible."

Before they left, Gil pulled me aside and said, "For what it's worth, I agree with Mike about Sammy. She happens to be terrific. But I don't agree with him about the getting married part. I *don't* think you should get married. If you were marrying Sammy

71

for her money like you said, which in itself is a lousy reason, and now she's disinherited, then you have no reason at all to marry her, not even a lousy one. But I wouldn't leave her standing at the altar on Monday. Sammy deserves better than that. If I were you, I'd call her today and tell her."

"Jesus Christ, Gil, don't worry about it. Of course I'll call her. I'm not going to let Sammy go to the wedding Monday and find out there that I'm not showing up. I'll call her tonight. I promise."

"Good," said Gil, climbing into his Morgan. He started up the engine, made a sharp U-turn, and hollered from the other side of the street, "You know, this was kind of cute, driving all the way from New York to Martha's Vineyard for a couple of beers and a pair of earmuffs."

The last thing Mike Malloy yelled was, "So long, asshole."

I didn't call Sammy that night like I promised I would.

The next morning at breakfast, quaint Mrs. Hopkins asked me if I was ever going to get married. Her question startled me. Why would she ask that?

"Because if you ever do," she said, "I have something to show you."

She took me to a hidden entranceway off the dining room that led up some steeply curved stairs to a hideaway bedroom.

"This is our bridal suite. Isn't it adorable?"

"Yes," I replied, "it's adorable." And it was. Sammy would have loved it.

Sammy would have loved everything about Martha's Vineyard. The names were so great. Menemsha, Tisbury, Gay Head, West Chop. She would have loved the names. And she would have loved yesterday's ferryboat ride and the Hopkins House, and this warm and cozy hideaway bedroom.

It's funny that all I could think about was Sammy.

That afternoon I called a taxi and caught the last ferry back to

72

Woods Hole. I took another taxi to Falmouth, and a bus from there to Boston. When I arrived at Logan Airport, it was too late to take a plane anywhere, so I stayed up all night and talked to a reservations clerk.

"Where are you going?" he asked.

"Greenwich, Connecticut."

"How come?"

"I'm going to get married."

"Really! When?"

"Today!"

"No kidding! Now why would you want to do something like that?" he asked.

"Because I'm in love," I answered.

Like my sister used to say, sometimes life is a big so-what.

That's what I thought when I saw the Wilkerson mansion again. It's nothing but a big so-what, I said to myself, and rang the doorbell.

The butler let me in and seemed surprised to see me. He said he didn't expect me until later that afternoon, at the wedding.

I told him that I wanted to hug and kiss Samantha, and I asked him where she was. He told me she was in her room getting dressed.

Halfway up the stairs I ran into Mrs. Wilkerson's secretary coming down. She blanched when she saw me.

"Where are *you* going?" she gasped.

"To see Sammy."

"You can't do that," she said, moving to block my way. "She's dressing. She's putting on her wedding gown. Does Mrs. Wilkerson know you're here?"

"No, she doesn't."

"Well, I don't know what to say," she said, still blocking my way. "Why can't you wait to see Samantha at the wedding?"

"Because I want to hug and kiss her right now," I said, pushing by Mrs. Wilkerson's secretary. She turned and chased after me for one or two steps, changed her mind, and dashed downstairs.

I knocked on Sammy's door and walked in.

She was standing in the middle of the room in her slip. Her wedding dress was spread out on her bed. When she saw me her eyes filled with tears, and she said, "I *knew* you'd come, you old fart," and then she ran into my arms and hugged me and kissed me.

"You know something?" I said, squeezing Sammy with all my might. "I love you. I really do."

"I could have told you that months ago," said Sammy, still crying. And then she said, "Can I ask you a very important question?"

"Absolutely. What is it?"

"Will we live happily ever after?"

"You bet your ass we will."

"Promise?" she asked.

"I promise."

"I guess you'll say anything to get me in bed with you." And then she laughed, and I laughed, and I was so happy I didn't know what to do. So I just held Sammy as tightly as I could, and that's when her mother charged into the room.

"*What* are *you* doing here!" she screeched.

Without letting Sammy go, I said I was hugging and kissing her daughter.

"Well, you leave right now. You just leave this instant, do you hear? It's bad enough that I have to see you this evening. I *do not* have to see you now. This is outrageous and I will *not* tolerate it. Are you listening to me? I said I will not tolerate this sort of behavior in my house, and if—"

"Mother," Sammy interrupted, still holding me in her arms.

"What?"

"Go to hell!"

Part 2

"**Y**ou can't *do* this to me. I just got married two weeks ago!" I said to the vice-president in charge of sales for the Transamerica Cuing Machine Company. The vice-president had called me into his office to tell me that I was going to spend all of my time as a traveling salesman.

"Listen," said the vice-president, lighting the butt of a half-chewed, half-smoked cigar. "Lotsa guys gotta do lotsa strange things if they want to get ahead in this world. You won't be the first traveling salesman who doesn't see his old lady for months on end, and you sure as hell ain't gonna be the last."

He paused to get his chewed-up cigar burning. When it was finally lit, he continued. "Look at it this way, buddy-boy. It's a way for you to get a name for yourself here at Transamerica. You make a couple of sales, and next year, who knows? And here's the *best* part. I was savin' this. You're in for a raise. Fifteen big ones a week! *And* an expense account. Fifteen bucks a week raise, and twenty bucks a day for expenses. *Plus* a company station wagon!"

"Who pays for the gas?" I asked.

"You."

"Out of *what?*"

"Out of your expense account," answered the vice-president.

"Where am I driving? I mean, what's my territory?"

"All over the country. The country is your territory, buddy-boy. What more can you ask for? A lotta guys would give their eyeteeth to be in your shoes."

"I'm not a lotta guys. I'm me, and I just got married two weeks ago!"

"Listen, ol' friend," said the vice-president, examining the end of his saliva-mangled cigar. "You may be just you, but you have no choice. Either you go on the road or you're fired and someone else will do it. I'll give you tonight to think about it. Go home and discuss it with the little woman."

"Thank you," I said, getting up to leave.

"Oh, one other thing," said the vice-president. "If you take the job, you better sell cuing machines."

"Can I take my wife with me?" I asked.

"Hell, no!" answered the vice-president.

"Who says so?" asked my sister Geraldine on the telephone.

"*He* says so! The vice-president in charge of sales says so," I answered. I was in a panic, so on my way home from the office I stopped in Mimi's and called my sister collect. "He says I'm not allowed to take Sammy with me."

"Who cares *what* he says? He's not going to be in the same car with you, is he? Just take Sammy along and have a ball. You'll see the country and enjoy the sights together. It'll be like one long honeymoon. Remember, two can live as cheap as one."

"That's true," I said.

"What a great way to start a marriage, Tommy. You're a lucky duck."

"It's a disaster!" I said to Sammy.

We were standing on the pavement in front of a television station in Youngstown, Ohio. Next to us were endless cases of Transamerica cuing machines. It was snowing, and our station wagon had been towed away because of a parking violation.

"It's a disaster," I repeated.

"It is *not*," said Sammy.

"But I don't even know where the station wagon *is!*"

"Who *cares?*" said Sammy, pulling my overcoat collar together.

"Who *cares?* I care, *that's* who cares. I just can't see us spending the rest of our lives in Youngstown, Ohio."

"As long as it's you and me, babe, we can spend the rest of our lives *anywhere!*" said Sammy.

"Anywhere?" I asked.

"Anywhere," my Sammy answered.

I turned out the light in our Wheeling, West Virginia, motel room and climbed under the covers. Sammy rolled over on her side and pulled my ear.

"Thomas, can I ask you something?"

"Sure," I said, burrowing my head into my pillow.

"Thomas, do you love me?"

"Okay, what's up, Sammy?" I asked.

"Nothing," she answered. "Just answer me. Do you love me?"

"Of course I do."

"Do what?"

"*Love* you."

"Thomas, do you know what the word 'love' means?"

"Yes."

"Well," said Sammy, "if you know what the word means, and you say you love me, then I guess you really do."

"Right," I said, half asleep.

Sammy rolled over and stared at the ceiling.

"Christ," she said to herself, "he'll say *anything* to get me in bed with him."

It was seven o'clock in the morning in Salt Lake City, Utah.

Sammy woke me up by poking me with short little four-fingered jabs to my rib cage. She was standing beside the bed holding a cupcake with a candle stuck in the middle. She had on

79

her pajamas, my bulky black overcoat, and my red woolen hat with the blue pompom. She looked absolutely ridiculous.

Then she started singing.

"Happy birthday to you. Happy birthday to you. Happy birthday, dear Thomas. Happy birthday to you."

Then she pulled me out of bed and put me over her knees. She smacked my backside twenty-six times, and once for good luck.

Then she kissed me.

"Wow," she said. "Twenty-six! You really *are* an old fart."

"Very funny," I said.

She gave me a present. It was an atrocious tie clip that had LOVE SAMMY engraved on its back. I still have it.

"How do you like it?" she asked, beaming.

"It's beautiful," I fibbed.

Then we climbed back into bed and made love. It was one of the nicest birthdays of my life.

"I've got a new system," I told Sammy, driving away from Helena, Montana, and heading toward the mountains.

"Where's all the equipment?" she asked.

"It's back at the television station."

"What's it doing back there?" asked Sammy. "Why aren't you with it? Why aren't we at the station setting it up?"

"Because," I said proudly, "*that's* my new system!"

"*What's* your new system?"

"I'm glad you asked," I said. "First of all, what's a chief engineer of a television station *hate* the most when I come knocking on his door? Answer: He hates to hear my sales pitch. *Anybody's* sales pitch. Okay, next question. What's a chief engineer *like* to do the most? Answer: Examine new equipment of any kind. He loves gadgets and he loves to play with them, at his leisure, with nobody over his shoulder pumping a sales pitch into his ear. So what's my new system? Simply this. From now on I'm going to dump the good old Transamerica cuing machines at the station and tell the chief engineer that the equipment speaks for itself. I'll tell him to play with it, examine it, put it on his cameras, use the machines on a show, whatever. And then I'll tell him that I'll be back at the end of the day to pick the equipment up and find out how he likes it. What do you think of that?"

"Honey," said Sammy, "if *you* like your new system, then I like your new system."

"Besides," I said, "it gives us more time to look around. It gives us a chance to smell flowers and climb mountains and look at trees and lay in meadows. What's wrong with that?"

"Absolutely nothing," answered Sammy.

We drove farther and farther away from town.

"Where are we going now?" asked Sammy.

"Swimming."

"Swimming?"

"Yes," I answered. "We are going swimming in the Missouri River."

"My hero," sighed my Sammy.

"Really?"

"Sure," said Sammy. "I'd much rather you play with me than with a bunch of boring television station executives."

"Exactly," I said, heading for the ol' Missouri.

It happened in Vancouver, British Columbia.

"Honey," said my Sammy in the middle of the night, "wake up." She was poking her four fingers into my rib cage.

"Why?" I asked in a daze.

"Because I think there's a snake in our bed," she answered demurely.

"There's a what in our bed?" I asked, only half awake.

"I said, I think there's a snake in our bed. I just had a dream that the two of us were running across a field. Suddenly I felt something cold and slimy on my leg. I shook my foot and a snake fell off. Then I woke up. But it was such a vivid dream that I'm not sure it *was* a dream. I really think there's a snake under the covers with us."

"Sammy," I said, now fully awake and getting angry. "This kind of joke isn't funny, particularly on a week night. I'll be tired tomorrow morning, and that means I'll be cranky. And *you* know, and I know—"

"I won't move a muscle," said Sammy, staring at the end of the bed, where our four sets of toes made four sets of bumps in the covers. "I won't breathe. I'll just sit rigid. You slide out of bed, slowly, and then jerk the covers back *fast.*"

"I will *not!*" I said with authority. "I'm twenty-six, going on thirty, and I'm *not* going to pull the covers back and look for a snake you *dreamt* about. We're adults, not children. Now go to sleep." I rolled over and closed my eyes.

Sammy remained rigid.

"I can't believe you," she said. "You're supposed to *protect* me. That was in the vows. Remember that part? Now *please,* get up and pull the covers back *quick!*"

"Jesus, Mother, Mary and Joseph," I growled.

I got up and pulled the covers back quick.

There was a snake in our bed.

It was a little green and white snake, about eight inches long. When I saw it I became numb with fear.

Sammy trapped the snake in a wastebasket and threw it out of the cabin. Then she climbed back in bed, fluffed up her pillow, and plopped her head into it. She pulled the blankets up so that just the top of her head stuck out.

"Come on, Frank Buck, get in bed. You'll catch cold if you stay out there all night."

I got under the covers and lay down, wide-eyed. Sammy put her arm around my stomach and said, "My hero." She giggled.

"Very funny."

"Don't worry," she said. "I'll protect you. It's in the contract, remember?"

I didn't answer, but I kissed her forehead.

"We can do it," I told Sammy.

"We can *not*," she said.

The two of us were trying to decide if our budget would allow a dinner at Ernie's Restaurant. Ernie's was posh *and* expensive. It had two waiters and a captain for every table. It also had red velvet walls.

"This place has red velvet walls, honey!" whispered Sammy.

"So?"

"So? So that means dinner is going to cost us an arm and a leg."

"We can afford it once in a while," I said, with the tone of a chaplain addressing his flock.

"We can *not*," replied my flock, "and we don't just do it once in a while. We *still* haven't recovered from that dinner we had in Denver. The expense account just won't take it."

"Yes it will," I said, knowing the expense account wouldn't take it.

"It *won't!*" said Sammy. She had worked it out so that we could live on our twenty-dollar-a-day expense account *if* I didn't interfere. And if we *did* live by her budget, we could mail my entire weekly pay check to our savings account in New York.

"*Please!*" said my Sammy, sounding like a trapped housewife pleading with a rapist. "We can make up our Denver losses by the end of this week, and if you butt out, we can put next week's pay check in the bank. Come on, sweetheart, we don't need red velvet walls. And besides, I'm not hungry. All I really want is a cheeseburger."

"Sammy, we're going to eat here, and that's that. We've been living on the road for months now, and I'm getting sick and tired of seeing you eat that rotten motel crap night after night. Anyway, you haven't visited San Francisco unless you've eaten at Ernie's."

"Who said so?" growled Sammy. Sometimes she could be a real pain in the ass.

We were seated in a booth near the kitchen, close to a container that the waiters threw dirty dishes into.

"Don't worry about the prices," I said to Sammy. "Just pick out what you want and order it."

"Okay, honey," she said, leaning back into the soft leather of our booth. "Like your grandmother used to say, if you're going to be fucked and there's nothing you can do about it, you might as well lay back and enjoy it."

I told Sammy that, to my knowledge, my grandmother never said that, and opened the menu. I saw the prices and felt faint. I looked for the cheapest thing I could find. When I found it, I didn't know what it was. The waiter had to translate for us, which was odd, considering we were still in the United States.

The check came to a little over seventy-three dollars.

"Jesus, Mother, Mary and Joseph," I said when we got outside.

"Well, you know what they say," said Sammy.

"No. What *do* they say?"

"You haven't seen San Francisco unless you've eaten at Ernie's."

That night, before we went to bed, I told Sammy, "One of these days we're not going to have to worry about the prices on menus."

"That's a shame," said my Sammy, pulling the covers up to her forehead. "I kind of like it the way it is."

We walked out of the Neiman-Marcus department store in Dallas, Texas, and Sammy fainted.

She looked at me, smiled, and said, "I think I'm going to faint," and fainted. Trying to catch her was like trying to catch a bowlful of jello. She just slithered through my arms and fell quietly to the sidewalk.

"Sammy, is there anything wrong?" I asked somewhat academically. I bent down and poked her stomach with my fingers. "Sammy, what's the matter?"

"She's fainted," said a kindly gray-haired woman with a warm smile. "Your wife has fainted."

A man offered to drive us to a hospital. The gray-haired lady suggested we go home instead.

"We're from out of town," I said. "We're staying at the Hilton Hotel."

A small crowd gathered and stood silently, shoulder to shoulder, staring at Sammy lying in a heap on the sidewalk.

The man who had offered to drive Sammy to the hospital said that he would take us to the Hilton. He helped me lift Sammy up. She opened her eyes. Beads of sweat were all over her face. "I think I fainted," she said softly.

"You're going to be fine," said the kindly gray-haired woman.

The man and I walked Sammy to a nearby parking lot and the elderly lady tagged along. When the man left to fetch his car, the lady took his place under Sammy's left arm. She leaned behind Sammy and said to me, "Your wife's pregnant."

"Pregnant!" I gasped.

"Yes." The woman smiled. "I can tell. I can *always* tell."

Two hours later, the Hilton Hotel house doctor diagnosed Sammy's fainting spell as acute food poisoning. I wasn't sure whether I was relieved that Sammy wasn't pregnant, or disappointed.

When the doctor left, I pulled a chair over to the side of Sammy's bed and sat down. She looked pale and drawn but, strangely enough, very pretty.

"Sammy," I said, "you're so beautiful, it's sickening."

She smiled and threw up.

"Oh, my God," I gulped, at four o'clock in the afternoon, in Tucson, Arizona. "Do you know what day this is?"

"No," said Sammy. "What day *is* this?"

85

"It's November the eighteenth!"

"So?"

"So," I said, "it's your birthday!"

"I *know!*" moaned Sammy, bursting into tears. "It's a hell of a time to remember. The goddamn day is almost over."

"Jesus, Sammy, you know how hard it is to keep track of the days when you're on the road."

"I kept track enough to know when it was *your* birthday. I woke you up at seven in the morning with a cake and candles."

"It was a *cup*cake with *one* candle."

"So what? It represented a whole cake and lots of candles. Anyway, I remembered at seven in the morning, *not* at four in the afternoon."

I took Sammy in my arms and kissed the top of her head. "Come on, Sammy," I said. "Stop crying. You know I hate to see you cry."

She stopped crying and blew her nose.

"So what did you buy me?"

"Oh, my God!" I gulped again.

"You didn't buy me *anything!*" she said, her eyes welling up all over the place.

Sammy's twentieth birthday is not one of my fondest memories.

Sammy was floating on an inner tube, talking to me from under her armpit. "Thomas, there's something about your system that makes me nervous."

"Like what?"

"Like the two of us are lying here on these inner tubes in the swimming pool of the Sands Hotel in Las Vegas, drinking gin and tonics, and wine, and somebody's paying you a weekly salary *plus* twenty dollars a day expense money."

"So?"

"So it's three o'clock in the afternoon and we've been floating

86

and drinking since eleven this morning, and somebody's paying you a weekly salary *plus* twenty dollars a day expense money."

"What's your point, Sammy?"

"Well," she said, "it's just too good to be true. We've hiked up mountains in Oregon, we've gone swimming in the Missouri River, seen Disneyland, Tijuana, Yellowstone, the Rockies. It's been the world's longest vacation, and you keep getting *paid* for it!"

She lifted her head up and rested her chin on the palm of her hand.

"It just seems to me," she continued, "that you should be doing something more than simply leaving the good old Transamerica cuing machines at the stations so the engineers can play with them. Maybe you should be in there giving a sales pitch instead of lying on an inner tube."

"Sammy," I said, pulling myself to the edge of the pool so I could take a sip of my gin and tonic. "If I've told you once, I've told you a thousand times, we have absolutely nothing to worry about."

The next day I was fired.

"What does it say?" asked Sammy. The it she was referring to was a night letter from the Transamerica Cuing Machine Company. I read it to her.

"It says that I am derelict in my duties. It says that the last six stations they called, the equipment was there, but I wasn't. It says that this will serve to terminate our relationship, to turn in the station wagon, and to ship the equipment back to New York."

"You weren't derelict, honey," said my Sammy. "They just didn't understand your system."

During the flight back to New York, Sammy hoisted a glass of wine and said, "Cheers, Thomas. You have nothing to be ashamed of. You stuck it out for an entire year with that ridiculous company. True, you devised a rather ingenious 'system' to make life infinitely more interesting, but nonetheless, you stuck it out. You didn't quit; they *fired* you. That's far more honorable than being branded a quitter."

Sammy certainly had a way of saying things.

"And besides," she went on, "the whole thing's a blessing in disguise. We've been on the road for almost a year. We've saved about seven thousand dollars and seen the United States from coast to coast. We've gotten to know each other and love each other, and we've had the time of our life. I'll bet we'll always look back to this past year with the good old Transamerica Cuing Machine Company as being one of the happiest years of our lives, and we're getting out while we're ahead. Cheers, Thomas, and I love you."

"I love you, too, Sammy," I said, and boy, did I.

"Where the hell have you been?" shouted my sister on the telephone.

"You know where we've been. I wrote you postcards."

"Post*card.* Singular, you craphead. I got one lousy postcard from you. Sammy was the one who wrote us all the time."

"Well, if you knew where Sammy was, you knew where I was, right?"

I think my sister was born hostile.

"How many kids do you have now?" I asked.

"Since I saw you, I had another son and a scare last Thursday. I've really missed seeing your stupid face. We're having a big New Year's Eve party. Why don't you and Sammy come? I've got to run. I think one of the boys fell in the toilet."

It was nice to be home. Even the old shithouse apartment looked good. And I was happy to see Gil Mack and red-faced Mike Malloy, and drink watered-down Scotch at Mimi's crummy restaurant again.

"I missed you," Mimi told Sammy, while he placed a double J&B and soda with a twist in front of me.

"I missed you, too, Sam," said Malloy. He had his big bearlike arm draped around her shoulders. Its weight pushed her chin almost down to the bar.

"Didn't anybody miss me?" I asked.

Everybody said no.

Gil told me that while we were gone, he had made a thousand-dollar bet with Mike. "One night, in here," said Gil, "Malloy said that he could stop drinking anytime he wanted to if he *really* wanted to. Mike said that when the chips were down, he had will power. I bet him a hundred bucks he wouldn't last a week."

"So I said, 'I'll go you one better,' " interrupted Malloy. "I said, 'I'll bet you a *thousand* dollars that I can stop for thirty days and nights,' and Gil took the bet."

"So did I," said Mimi. "I bet Mike five bucks that he wouldn't last out the *night!*"

"I was on the honor system," said Malloy. "If I sneaked one somewhere, I was bound by honor to admit it and pay off."

Mimi said that Gil and Mike each gave him a check, right then and there, for a thousand dollars made out to each other, and he kept the checks in his cash register.

"I went to Saint Patrick's Cathedral," said Gil, "and lit a candle. I said a prayer. I said, 'Dear God, if Malloy cheats and doesn't tell me, make him impotent.' "

Malloy boomed out a laugh and doubled over on his stool, making Sammy's chin actually touch the bar.

"You never told me that," he roared.

"I was afraid to," said Gil Mack.

"What the hell were you doing in Saint Patrick's?" Sammy asked Gil. "You're not even Catholic."

"So what," said Gil. "It doesn't make any difference as long as you make a donation."

"The bet started on November first," said Malloy, with his arm still draped over Sammy's shoulders, "and I didn't have a drop of booze for an entire month. Not a drop. And it changed me. I stopped fooling around after work. I came right home, played with the kids, talked things over with Mary, and went to bed early. I took Mary out to dinner once a week, and I took Mary and the kids to church on Sundays. The priests didn't recognize me. They thought Mary was a widow."

Mike ordered another round of drinks. Sammy had a Coke. When the drinks came, Mike downed half of his in one swallow and continued. "I watched television at night with a cup of Sanka on my lap. I woke up every morning fresh as a daisy, and made such good decisions at the bank the executive vice-president started looking at me with a mixture of awe and worry. Suddenly I was a threat to his job. Also, I lost ten pounds and some of the flush in my face."

"I don't think I would have liked you that way," Sammy said quietly.

"*Nobody* liked me!" howled Malloy. "I was a goddamned bore. My resistance went down and I caught one cold after another. My family couldn't adjust to my being home at night. Mary began looking at me suspiciously, and the kids were always tense. About two weeks into the bet, my wife offered to pay half, out of her savings, if I'd start drinking right away."

Gil said, "Every once in a while, after work, we'd meet and have dinner together. We'd just eat and stare at each other."

"And *this* place was like a morgue," said Mimi. "With Malloy on the wagon, this place was like a goddamn morgue."

"But I stuck it out," boasted Mike, "and on the night of December first, I walked in here, picked up my checks, and tied on the biggest drunk of my life."

"He punched some poor bastard in the mouth and knocked out three of the guy's teeth," said Mimi, with a fond expression on his face. "For no reason at all, he punched the bastard in the mouth."

"No reason, hell," bellowed Malloy. "He was hassling you all night, Mimi."

"That was no reason to knock three of his teeth out," said Mimi warmly.

"The poor cat fell under my piano," said Jack-the-Piano-Player, "and he just laid there. I played all of 'Sunny Side of the Street' and 'Don't Get Around Much Anymore' before he opened his eyes."

"Mike, you're my favorite Irishman," said Sammy. Malloy kissed her cheek loudly and knocked over his drink with his fat arm.

That night, while he was driving home, Mike Malloy's car hit a tree. Mike went through his front windshield, head first. He died instantly.

It was a shitty Christmas.

Sammy and I, and Gil, spent the day with Mike Malloy's family at their home in Middletown, New Jersey. When I stepped into their hallway, Mike's youngest son ran up to me, put his hands around my waist, and cried into my stomach. His big fat tears made dark stains on my suit.

I held Mike's wife Mary in my arms. Mike had once told me that Mary was the best friend he ever had. And then I remembered Woods Hole, and Malloy, all flushed with whiskey, his thick neck bulging over his collar, his tie down and the top of his shirt unbuttoned, saying, ". . . and that's why I think Sammy is so great. She'll be the best friend Tommy ever had."

"I'll miss that red-faced bastard," said Mike's wife. I told her I would, too.

"Mike Malloy's lying dead in a box," said Gil on our way home. "He has no more value to us. He's now worth about as much as a dead ant, or a dead fly, or Napoleon, or Tolstoy, or a dead dog that you see lying on the side of the road. When you step on a cockroach, the cockroach is dead. Just like Malloy."

Silent night. Holy night. All is calm. All is bright.

Should auld acquaintance be forgot. . .

"How's your mother and father, Samantha?" asked a very

toothy and aristocratic female at Geraldine's New Year's Eve party.

"I haven't the slightest idea," answered Samantha, looking into her ginger ale. "I haven't spoken to them for almost a year."

And never brought to mind . . .

"What are you doing now, Tommy?" asked the toothy aristocrat's totally uninterested husband.

"I'm with the CIA."

Should auld acquaintance be forgot . . .

"Are you supposed to tell people you're with the CIA?" asked the husband, showing a glimmer of concern.

"Not really. But I know you can keep a secret."

And auld lang syne.

"What's bothering you, Thomas?" asked my Sammy in a relatively uncrowded hallway.

"These people bother me."

"Why?"

"Because they're gloating over your disinheritance and my unemployment. They're pushing our noses into it and enjoying the whole goddamn thing."

"Don't worry about it, honey."

"I'm not, Sammy, because I'm going to succeed. I'm going to become a rich son of a bitch, and when I do I'm going to come home and kick their asses all the hell over Connecticut."

"My hero."

For auld lang syne, my dear, For old lang syne . . .

"Sammy, it's nice to see you," said a diamond-bedecked dowager. "How's your brother? I understand he's married now."

"He is?"

We'll take a cup o' kindness now . . .

The man spoke to me through his cigar smoke. "I saw your father-in-law yesterday, Tommy. I don't think he knows you're home."

"I don't think he knows we're alive."

"I don't think that's a very nice thing to say," said the man, squinting his eyes.

"Who the bloody fuck gives a shit what you think is or isn't a nice thing to say?"

The man's hand, which was traveling to his mouth with his cigar, froze.

"Honey," said Sammy, slipping my arm around her shoulders, "let's go home."

For auld lang syne.

"Thomas, wake up!"

I woke up.

I looked at my watch. It was a little after three o'clock in the morning. Why did Sammy always get brainstorms at three o'clock in the morning?

"Thomas, let's go to Europe!"

I rolled over, amazed at how patient I had become. The trait was obviously acquired out of necessity.

"Thomas, wake up and turn on your light."

I didn't turn on my light.

"Thomas," continued Sammy, "if you had your choice of anything in the whole world that you could do, if you were able to have your favorite wish come true, you would go to Europe and write your book, wouldn't you? If a genie popped up at the foot of the bed right now and said, 'Tommy, what can I do for you?' you would beg him to let you go to Europe so that you could write your book. Isn't that right, Thomas? Isn't it?"

I didn't answer. It was after three o'clock in the morning and my wife was talking to me about genies. My metabolism couldn't cope, so I didn't answer.

"Honey, Mike Malloy wanted to go to Dublin and write his play. He always said that he didn't care if the play was a piece of shit or the next great Irish classic, as long as he could go to Dublin and write it, and get the play out of his system. Mike knew

93

the plot of that play backward and forward. Honey, Mike wanted to do so many things. He wanted to write his play. He wanted to write a movie. He even wanted to start a new dance craze. Remember?"

I didn't say a word. Long ago I learned that once you talk to Sammy when she wakes you in the wee hours of the morning, there's no telling when you'll ever go to sleep again.

My wife lit a cigarette and waved the smoke away with her hand. Sammy always waved the smoke away with her hand when she was excited.

"But of all the things he wanted to do," continued Sammy, fluffing up the pillows behind her back, "the thing he wanted to do most was to go to Dublin and write his play, just like you want to go to Europe and write your book. He dreamed of being the next Brendan Behan, just like you dream of being the next F. Scott Fitzgerald or the next Ernest Hemingway. And who knows, maybe Mike could have been, if only he had done it. Now he'll never get the chance. He's dead, and that's that."

I sat up and thought of Mike, and Mike's play. I knew the plot well. He had told it to me a dozen times. It was a good story, and Mike was a good writer. He *should* have written it.

"But he wouldn't have had to go all the way to Dublin to write it," I said. "He could have written his play at home on weekends, or in his office at night, instead of running around New York drinking himself to death."

"Then why do *you* want to go to Europe?" asked Sammy. "Because it's a dream of yours, that's why. So why not do it? Thomas, there's just a few times in your life when you're able to do that sort of thing, and now happens to be one of them. We have nothing to tie us down. Not a thing. No children, no job, nothing. And we have the money. We have our savings. Between your salary we saved all last year, and the cash we got when we were married, we must have over ten thousand dollars!"

"But why, Sammy?" I asked, somewhat excited and suddenly

wide awake. "Why take out all of our savings *now*, and go whipping around Europe while I write the Great American Novel. I'm twenty-six. I should be looking for a job instead of drifting from pillar to post. I should settle down and start making something of myself so that all the Wilkersons can stop patting each other on the back and doing a lot of I-told-you-sos about the bum their daughter married."

I fell into a sullen quiet.

"It was just a thought," Sammy said, sliding down under the covers. "It's just that I'm sure you could write a fine book. And in Europe you would be writing where you've always wanted to write the most. But maybe you're right. I guess if I were a man I would worry about things like what the Wilkersons would say, just like Mike Malloy worried about the executive vice-president of his bank. A lot of good all that worry's doing him now. Good night, Thomas. I'm exhausted."

Of course I never went back to sleep. Sometime between four and six I slid out of bed and went into the living room, where I could smoke my pipe and look out of our window at the roaming insomniacs and taxis on Third Avenue.

It was close to nine in the morning when Sammy came out to make coffee.

"When's our anniversary?" I asked.

"You should know that. It's January the tenth," she answered, putting on the hot water and yawning. "It's a week from tomorrow."

"Let's celebrate it in Europe."

"Just you and me, babe?" she asked with her back to me.

"Just you and me, babe."

Sammy turned around. Her smile ran from one ear to the other.

"It's warm, stale beer!" said Sammy when she tasted bitters for the first time. She smacked her lips loudly and made the same kind of face you make when you burp up something you ate six hours earlier.

"Hush up," I said in a low voice, looking furtively from side to side. "Do you want us to get the reputation of being ugly Americans?"

We had been in London exactly one week, and just as I promised, we were celebrating our first anniversary in Europe. But Europe was far from cheerful. It had rained steadily since we arrived, and it was cold; a raw, cutting cold that worked its way through your clothes and chilled you to the bone.

We spent our first night in a cheap hotel near Knightsbridge. The next day, in a driving rain, we looked for an apartment. We found one in a drab building on the corner of Shepherd and Carrington Streets. The flat was on the second floor, over a grocery store.

The apartment was unheated. We bought an electric heater but it didn't seem to help very much. We decided to buy another one. When we plugged the second heater into the wall, it overloaded the circuits and blew the lights out in the entire building. The landlord reprimanded us, so we stayed in bed a lot, and took hot baths a lot. It was the only way to avoid freezing to death.

When we weren't trying to keep warm, I would make feeble attempts to begin my book. I would arrange my papers and typewriter, and then rearrange them; then change tables, then change back again. I did everything but write. Sammy was watching but made out she wasn't. That's how it had been for a week. But today was different. It was our first wedding anniversary, and I was "taking the day off" to celebrate.

"Here's to us," chirped Sammy, smacking her halfpint of bitters against mine. We were sitting in the Old Chesterfield Pub, a warm, wooden, comfortable place just across the street from our refrigerated flat. We forced a lot of smiles and tried to convince each other that we were happy and adventurous, and doing the right thing.

"Here's to us," I said. "It's you and me, babe."

"Right," said Sammy, and we touched glasses again.

It's tough to be festive when you're worried.

"Hey, Sammy," I said with gusto. "I checked around and I found out that Mirabelle is the finest restaurant in London, and it's right up the street. I think it's only fitting that we celebrate our first wedding anniversary in the finest restaurant in London."

"You would, Thomas," she said. "Here we go again. When are you going to learn that I am *not* a gourmet, and that fancy restaurants grate me, they don't impress me."

We didn't eat at Mirabelle.

We had two cheeseburgers at Wimpy's. We sat on the same side of the booth and hugged and kissed. I caught the couple in the next booth watching us. They smiled sheepishly. The man had a gold tooth.

"Promise me you'll never have a gold tooth," Sammy whispered.

I promised.

Sammy and I went back to our apartment and took a hot bath together.

"Happy anniversary, you old fart," she said.

"Happy anniversary, honey."

"Do you still love me, after an *entire* year? Do you?" she asked.

"Yes, I really do."

"How do you know?"

"Because I know," I answered.

"Give me concrete proof."

"Because I'm holding you in my arms right now, even though you're wearing a shower cap. Did you ever see yourself in a shower cap?"

"It's not so good, is it?" Sammy asked.

"That's just it. If I can love you when you're wearing a shower cap, then that's concrete proof I can love you the rest of my life."

Sammy pulled her leg out of the water and examined it. "You

know," she said, "you could drown making love in a bathtub."

"You're right," I said, sliding down so that the water line stopped at my lower lip.

"Thank God English bathtubs are big enough to hold two people," said Sammy.

"Thank God," I repeated.

"Have you ever made love in a bathtub before?" asked Sammy.

"Before tonight? No, that was a first."

"Neither have I," she said matter-of-factly.

"I'm glad."

"You know, you really *could*," she said.

"Could what?"

"Could drown making love in a bathtub. I mean, there you were on top of me, your eyes closed tight with the excitement of it all—and mine were closed, too, of course—and the two of us thrashing around in the throes of violent passion and lust, like we were, and for all you knew my head could have been under water, and my thrashing could have been a need for air, not lust. I could see you opening your eyes and saying, 'My God, I've drowned the poor thing.' "

"True," I said, mesmerized by my toes at the end of the tub.

"That would make an interesting, if somewhat macabre, short story, don't you think? I think I'll write it."

"Hold it! I'm the writer in this family," I said.

"When are you starting?" she asked.

"Soon," I answered.

Our bed was colder than ever. Only the center was bearable. The sides were like two ice floes. Sammy and I huddled in the middle, a ball of arms and legs, trying to warm each other by pressing together as hard as we could.

I heard Sammy's voice somewhere under my chin. "We've both been afraid to talk about it," she said, "but have you noticed that I haven't had one single asthma attack since we've been married?"

"I've noticed," I said. "Let's not talk about it."

"And my eye doesn't twitch anymore, and I haven't had any liquor since our wedding. Have you noticed that, too?"

"Yes, I've noticed that, too."

"I'd say that you've been rather a good influence on my life, you old fart."

"It's about time that dawned on you."

"My hero," Sammy said, and fell asleep on my arm. I held onto her for dear life. It was one of the coldest anniversaries we would ever share. It was also one of the best.

My father died.

I found out by cable on a rainy Sunday morning. The boy who delivered the telegram waited by the door for a tip. He had very red cheeks and a runny nose. I read the message, and as I read it, I closed the door slowly in the boy's face.

"What does it say?" asked Sammy.

"It's from Ma. It says, 'Dad died last night. It's a blessing. Funeral tomorrow. Don't come home. Good luck with the book. Love to Sammy.' And it's signed, 'Mother.' "

I wasted all of the following day in the Old Chesterfield Pub, forcing down gallons of lukewarm beer and dragging my memory for father-son pictures. I was surprised at how few there were.

By midafternoon I convinced myself that my father had taken to his grave the conviction that his son was, and always would be, a bum. I had done nothing to jar that conviction, had I? Hadn't death left him with a picture of me loafing around Europe, living off the wedding money of my disinherited ex-heiress wife? Once a bum, always a bum—deedle, deedle, dumpling, my son Tommy.

Just before the pub closed for the night, I went to the men's room and threw up. I remember so clearly leaning against a chalk-white wall, staring at my vomit in the toilet bowl, and crying.

I think that was my all-time low.

"Thomas, wake up."

"I'm up."

"I know you are."

It was four o'clock in the morning. I hadn't slept a wink. I hadn't the night before, either.

"Thomas, let's go to the south of France, where it's warm and cheerful and sunny. When you're not writing, we can sit at outdoor cafés and watch the world go by. There's no law that says we have to stay here, is there?"

"No."

Sammy lit a cigarette and waved away the smoke with her hand.

"Then why are we fighting it? Let's get up and pack right now. We can leave by the time the sun comes up."

"By the time the *what* comes up?" It had been raining steadily for two weeks.

Sammy corrected herself. "By the time the dawn comes up."

Looking back at number 12 Shepherd Street from the rear window of our taxi, I wondered why we had stayed as long as we had.

"Where shall we go?" asked Sammy on the way to the airport.

"Let's start with Nice."

"Nice, on the French Riviera," sighed Sammy. "I guess you'll promise just about *anything* to get me in bed with you."

Rolling down the runway, Sammy slipped her hand in mine. She always did. She usually kept it there until the seat belt sign went off.

"Ciao, London," she said, waving backward with her other hand.

"Why are you crying?" I asked.

"Because we had such a good time there," she answered.

It was raining in Nice.

We rented a car and drove to Saint Tropez.

The rain never stopped. It came down in thick, wet waves that exhausted the windshield wipers. We drove through enchanting seaport towns, and past magnificent villas whose beauty should have impressed us, but it didn't. The downpour was breaking our backs. It was washing away the last remnants of our cheer and confidence.

Most of the stores and hotels in Saint Tropez were closed for the winter, their green and gray shutters tightly latched.

We found a bleak, dank room in a colorless pension. I killed a cockroach before Sammy noticed it and felt terribly depressed about its being there. The room was cold, just like our room in London. I had forgotten how it felt to be warm.

I became irritable. The weather bothered me. The pension bothered me. The huge wad of French francs that bulged out of my inadequate wallet bothered me. Europe was a drag.

The only restaurant that was open reeked of hostility, or so it seemed. All the locals watched us walk in and followed us with their eyes until we sat down. Some kept staring even after we were seated. All the men want to rape Sammy, I thought to myself, and all the women are laughing because they think I'm funny-looking.

"We're going home," I announced abruptly to Sammy.

"When?" she asked calmly.

"Tomorrow!"

"Okay," said Sammy. "I'm with you, babe."

When I went to bed that night, I felt terribly sorry for myself. I was depressed about the money we had wasted and the book I would never write. I fell asleep angry, and dreamed a series of short bothersome dreams until Sammy woke me in the morning.

"Look!" she hollered. "Look at the beautiful sunshine!"

I went to the window and stood beside her. Outside the air was cold and crisp, but not chilling. A clear breeze blew across Saint Tropez, and brought with it springtime smells. The town, with its yellow and pink buildings and orange Spanish-tiled roofs, looked like a giant watercolor painting. The Mediterranean was a spar-

101

kling blue, and the harbor swayed with the masts of a hundred boats of all sizes. Children chattered and yelled in a nearby school, and a church tower bonged eight o'clock. Under us, motorbikes whizzed past and women carried long, thin loaves of bread in wicker baskets.

"Sammy."

"Yes, dear."

"Let's find a place to live, and stay awhile."

Our apartment was on the top floor of a four-story building that jutted out from the corner of the harbor. The building was as close to the sea as you could get. When our windows were open, the apartment was filled with the sound of waves rolling back and forth over the yellow rocks below.

The window in our living room was high enough to clear the top of an antiquated lighthouse next door, giving us a wonderful view of the Mediterranean. In the morning we would watch the fishing boats going out to sea, and at nights we could see the twinkling blue and white lights of Sainte Maxime across the bay.

The apartment was cheerful and warm, even when it rained, sometimes more so when it rained. Sammy would often pick a rainy day to experiment with her French cooking, and the smells would drift through the apartment, making me ravenously hungry hours before dinner was ready.

Outside, the rain would kick up the sea, and white-capped waves would hit the rocks harder than usual, and sea gulls would sometimes hang suspended, trying to fly upstream against the heavy winds. Still, the Mediterranean never seemed ominous; just aggressive enough to make you happy to be inside with all the lamps lit, and the soft pillows and comforters, and the good music, and the mouth-watering smell of Sammy's cooking.

On sunny days Sammy and I would drive into the countryside for lunch, or explore the Plage Salin, or the Plage Tahiti, or perhaps one of the smaller beaches along the coastline. Most often we would just sit in a restaurant on the waterfront and watch the people go by.

Our favorite outdoor café was the Senequir, with its red tables and chairs, and its equally colorful crowd that gathered every day to sit in the sunshine. For some of the Senequir bunch, staring at the sun was a pleasant way to spend a restful lunch hour. For others, it was an occupation.

Before the tourists arrived, most of the faces never changed at the Senequir. We would always see the same people tilted back in their chairs, eyes closed, facing the sun: the hired help from the nearby hotels, the rich mother and daughter, the poor dock worker and fisherman, the double-chinned, sixty-year-old retired wealthy merchant with his pretty twenty-year-old German wife.

And there was always the wastrel son, sitting with other wastrel sons and daughters, whose daily excitement would come with the arrival of a new Rolls-Royce in town, or a new yacht anchoring in the harbor.

But the wastrels were always friendly, and so were the hotel clerks, and the fisherman, and the double-chinned merchant and his wife. Everyone would say, *"Bonjour, monsieur et madame. Comment ça va?"* and I would grin and wave because I didn't know how to answer them. Sammy and I could hardly speak a word of French, and what I spoke was generally incorrect.

"Bonjour," I said to Madame Borchardt, our landlady, one night as we were leaving the apartment.

"Honey, you said good *morning* to Madame Borchardt," Sammy told me when we got outside. "You said good morning to her, and it's nine o'clock at night! *Bonjour* is good morning. *Bonsoir* is good evening. You always get them mixed up."

I did. I would say good evening to the mailman in the morning when he arrived, and hello when he left. When I met someone on the street, I would confidently shake his hand and say good-bye.

Sammy learned the language immediately. Her favorite word

103

was *merde*, meaning shit. If she didn't like someone, she would call him a *merde*head. I don't think that was the proper use of the word, but then who was I to say?

When Sammy and I first came to Saint Tropez, most of the stores were closed and the harbor was practically empty. Now almost all the shops were open for business, and the waterfront slips were filling up with yachts and schooners from all over the world. The *Malle-Nostrum* from Toulon, the *Santa Cruz* from Barcelona, the *Cathy-Ann II* out of Panama, the *Avis,* the *Colibri,* the *Ariel,* the *Illusion.*

In June the tourists arrived, and in August the French. The two of us seemed to sense how fast time was going by. "We're living the good life," Sammy once said. "We make love in the rain and walk in the sun." She may have been slightly dramatic, but she was right. We *were* living the good life, and we were enjoying every minute of it.

And I was playing the role of author to the hilt.

I had taken to drinking Pernod because Hemingway did, and I had grown a beard because Hemingway did. I secretly hated the Pernod *and* the beard. The Pernod gave me heartburn and the beard itched, but I wouldn't admit either to Sammy.

And I was also getting fat.

It was Sammy's French cuisine that was doing it.

"I'm fat!" I would bellow periodically.

"You are not," Sammy would reply. "You're just pleasingly plump." And then she would place roast chicken with peaches, covered in a wine sauce, in front of me, and mounds of French bread, and caramel custard, and half a bottle of Beaujolais. And there was always a gathering of sweets from the local patisserie in the refrigerator. Little fragile lemon tarts, and eclairs, and cream puffs, and white meringue cookies with a cherry in the middle, and pigs' ears, and God knows what else.

Sometimes, early in the morning, when the streets were empty, I would drop twenty centimes into the scale in front of the Pharmacie du Port, and cringe until its big arm came to rest. I would quickly multiply the kilograms by 2.2 and go home in a bad mood.

"It's official, Samantha," I would say, as soon as I returned from the *pharmacie.* "I am now on a forty-eight-hour fast. Nothing but water for forty-eight hours. Do you understand that, Samantha? Nothing but water."

"Right," she would say happily. "Just do me a favor and start your fast *after* breakfast. I've made it already." And then she would serve me two eggs over, dropped gingerly on top of a thick juicy slice of fried ham, and more mounds of freshly baked bread, and gobs of butter and jam, and a huge pitcher of white wine.

"You're so considerate of my weight problem," I would say, when I finished eating and was unable to stand up.

"Don't worry about it, Thomas. It's you and me, babe, all the way."

"A thin you and a fat me."

"Who cares?" said Sammy.

Some nights I would wake up and look at Sammy, and wonder how anyone could be so beautiful, and so smart, and so warm. Sometimes I would love her so much I would hug and kiss her hard, and wake her up, and she would ask if there was anything wrong.

"No," I would say, "everything's fine. I just can't sleep because I ate too much."

And some nights I couldn't sleep for other reasons.

I would lie awake thinking of a discussion I had had with Roger Mouvant and Dominique Dejeneur at Lescale's one afternoon, over a glass of wine. Roger and Dominique were two journalists who had resigned from *Paris-Match* and gone to Spain to gather material for a novel they were going to write. They had returned to their homes in Saint Tropez a few months ago, and were busy getting their notes in order.

"Think of the hell Edward Hemma must have gone through,"

Roger Mouvant had said, "when the book he had spent four years working on never sold a copy."

"Ah, that *is* sad," said Dominique Dejeneur, "but unfortunately that is the nature of our profession. You must keep asking yourself, Does anybody care what I am writing? Will anybody be interested in what I have to say?"

I rolled over on my stomach and tried another position. I listened to Sammy breathing. She had a certain steady rhythm to her breathing when she was sleeping. You could hum a song to it.

You must keep asking yourself, Does anybody care what I am writing? Will anybody be interested in what I have to say?

Shit, no, I answered, almost out loud.

"What's the matter, honey?" asked Sammy, only half awake and full of halitosis. She always seemed to know when something was troubling me, even in her sleep.

"Nothing," I lied. "Go to sleep. It's two o'clock in the morning."

"So?" she said, sitting up and turning on her bed lamp.

"What do you mean, so?" I asked, relieved that she was up.

"So what if it's two o'clock in the morning? We're not on any schedule, are we? If you don't feel like sleeping now, you'll catch up tomorrow." She lit a cigarette and waved the smoke away with her hand. "What's bothering you? Tell me. Spit it out, you old fart. You don't break out in a sweat just because it's Thursday." She wiped her palm across my forehead and upper lip.

I told her what was bothering me. "And besides," I said, "we're going to run out of money, and *then* what'll we do? Who will we turn to? Look, let's just chalk it up to a happy experience and quit while we can still operate. Let's go home with whatever money we have left and use that money to cover us until I find a job. All we're doing is just setting ourselves up to get massacred six months from now."

"Like *hell* we are," Sammy said, dragging heavily on her cigarette.

She got out of bed and began pacing back and forth. "In other words, you want to take the last six months of our lives, drop them in the toilet, and flush them into the bay of Saint Tropez, right? Well, if that's what you want to do, then that's what we'll do. It's you and me, babe, but personally I think you're crazy. You're homesick, and insecure, and scared. You've got every right to be. But don't quit now. If you do, you'll never forgive yourself. You'll go home and get a job, and every day for the rest of your life you'll wonder. You'll wonder what would have happened if you had stayed two more months and finished your book. Maybe, just maybe, it might very well have *been* the Great American Novel. Wouldn't it kill you not to know?"

She smashed her cigarette into an ashtray and sat down on the edge of the bed.

"Thomas, finish it, and let it fail. At least you'll know, and you'll have no regrets. That's far better than eating your heart out for the rest of your life." She rubbed the covers where my toes were. "Someone said, 'I'll never regret the things I've done. I'll only regret the things I've never done.' Don't quit now, Thomas. Please. You'll have a lifetime to get nice safe nine-to-five jobs." And then she said she was hungry and went to the kitchen.

As usual, she was right. If there was one thing I hated, it was a nice safe nine-to-five job. At least I was doing something on my own. True, the odds against the book being a success were great, maybe overwhelming, but if it *did* succeed, if it *was* a best seller . . .

"Hey, Thomas, come keep me company," hollered Sammy through a mouthful of food.

I went into the kitchen and had orange juice, and eggs, and half a steak that was supposed to be for dinner that night, and ham, and a croissant, and a brioche, and cheese, and coffee. While we ate, the remnants of a wedding party passed under our window. We listened until their drunken harmonizing disappeared around the corner.

By the time we finished eating, it was almost six o'clock in the morning and the sun was coming up. Sammy went back to bed and fell asleep immediately. I just sat in a chair and watched her sleep. She was on her side, her hair spread over her shoulders, her hands tucked under the pillow.

I listened to her breathing. I hummed "Yankee Doodle" to it.

"Today is your birthday! Happy Birthday, Tommy," said Madame Borchardt, and Roger Mouvant, and Dominique Dejeneur, and Monsieur Lyon, and Felix Lescale and his wife, and Sammy.

It was a surprise birthday party for me at Lescale's restaurant that I had known about for over a week. The party was so badly organized that Sammy finally had to confess, and pleaded that I act surprised.

I pretended to be flabbergasted, and hugged and kissed everyone. There was a big birthday cake with twenty-eight candles—one was for good luck—and funny hats, and noisemakers, and streamers, and confetti. Everyone gave me a silly present, and Felix ordered the bartender to let me have free drinks all day long. It was a warm, boisterous party that lasted until three in the morning. Sammy put me to bed with tender loving care.

That night I had a dream. It should have been a happy one, but it wasn't. It was a nightmare.

I dreamed that a new yacht named *El Slicko* docked in Saint Tropez. It was a mammoth yacht painted entirely baby blue, and it was obviously named after its owner, who appeared to be a slick, lecherous-looking man of about fifty. He wore his black, greasy hair parted in the middle, and he had a pencil-thin mustache, just like the old-time matinee idols. The rake stood on the aft deck of his boat in a baby blue terry cloth robe, baby blue silk hose that came up to his knees, and baby blue patent leather shoes. He had his arms folded across his chest and did nothing but stare licentiously at a young girl sitting at an outdoor café across the street.

And then I noticed that the old libertine was making overly

exaggerated faces at the young girl, and that she was laughing uproariously. I saw nothing funny in the contorted expressions of El Slicko, and marveled at the reaction he was getting from the girl.

Soon she got up from her table and joined El Slicko on his boat. Later, they came out to the aft deck again. The young girl was wearing El Slicko's baby blue terry cloth robe, and obviously had nothing on underneath it. El Slicko was naked, except for his baby blue hose and shoes. He had his hairy arm around the young girl's shoulders, and he was still making his unfunny facial expressions, and the girl was still laughing uncontrollably.

That's how the boat sailed out of the harbor: El Slicko and the young girl standing together on the aft deck, waving good-bye to all of us sitting in the outdoor cafés. And just before the boat disappeared, I recognized the girl. It was my wife.

I woke up instantly and felt for Sammy. She was there, and I was relieved.

"Sammy, wake up."

"Why?"

"Because I said so."

"I don't want to wake up," she said.

"Well, wake up anyway. I always wake up when *you* say so."

"You're a fool," she muttered, slithering deeper into her covers.

"The *hell* I am. Now wake up."

"Why?" she asked again.

"Because I want to tell you something."

"What?" She still hadn't moved a muscle. She carried on our conversation as if she were temporarily paralyzed from head to foot.

"Sammy, look at me."

She turned painfully, with lots of sighing, until we were finally face to face. "I'll remember this, Sammy, the next time you wake *me* in the middle of the night."

"What is it you have to tell me?" she asked with her eyes shut.

"It's just this," I said, pausing for the necessary dramatic effect. "Don't ever leave me for another man."

The silence was deafening.

"Sammy, did you hear what I said?"

"*Yes,* I heard what you said. Honestly! *That's* what you woke me up to tell me. What time *is* it, Thomas?"

"It's four-fifteen, almost."

"You woke me at four-fifteen in the morning to tell me what you just told me? You know, Thomas, I really think you've been working too hard. Tomorrow you're going to stay in bed all day and I'm going to make you chicken soup."

"Come on, Sammy," I said. "Be serious for a minute."

"I will *not* be serious," said Sammy angrily. "I refuse to dignify that kind of question with an answer. Now good night, for Christ sake."

I said good night and went to sleep, content.

Toward the end of December, I grabbed Sammy in my arms and twirled her around and around in a circle.

"Guess what?" I shouted.

"What?"

"I've finished! I've finished the goddamn book!"

"Great!" Sammy whooped, and started crying.

"Now what the hell are you *crying* about?"

"I'm just so goddamn happy, that's all."

That night I decided to celebrate by allowing us to have dinner at Les Mouscardins. It was the best restaurant in Saint Tropez. It was also the most expensive.

"Jesus H. Christ," muttered Sammy, somewhat irreverently.

"What's wrong now?"

"When the hell are you going to learn that expensive restaurants—"

". . . grate me and do not impress me," I mimicked. I knew the lecture well.

"So?" said Sammy, her eyes two little slits, her mouth all squinched up, her hands on her hips.

"So just unfurrow everything and move along quietly. What are you so worried about? The book's going to be a best seller. You know that. *And* a smash Broadway musical, *and* a . . ."

We got seated and I ordered a bottle of wine. When it was poured, we touched glasses.

"Here's to the Great American Novel," I said.

"No!" said Sammy. "Here's to *us!* To our happiness and good health."

We drank to us.

"Okay to do the Great American Novel now?" I asked.

"Yes," said Sammy, smiling.

We drank to the Great American Novel.

"Will you be glad to get home?" I asked.

"Yes," said Sammy. "Will you?"

"You bet," I said firmly, but way down deep, I wasn't so sure.

Somewhere between four and five that morning, Sammy woke me and said, "Thomas, let's go to Paris and make a baby. It's on the way home and we've never been to Paris, and we've never made a baby."

And that's exactly what we did. We rented an old Citroën and drove to gay Paree.

Our baby was conceived in room 411 of the Hotel Saint Pierre. How do I know? Because Sammy said so.

"I'm not going to get myself all excited," I told her when we finished making love. "I'm going to wait until you take the rabbit test, or whatever you do to see if you're pregnant or not."

"Thomas," said Sammy, lighting a cigarette, "get excited."

"No doubts at all?"

"No doubts at all."

The Hotel Saint Pierre was just off the Boulevard Saint Germain, on the Left Bank of Paris. The Rue Pierre was no wider than an automobile, and a small one at that. When an American car came down the street, you would have to flatten yourself against a building much the same as the hero does in spy movies when he knows he's being followed.

The bed in our room was gigantic. So was the bathtub. Nothing else worked. Things were there only because tradition called for it. The drawers in the dresser were always stuck, the closet had no hangers, and the desk was too weak to write on. But the bed and bathtub functioned superbly. "After all," said the ancient bellhop, "that's all that counts, isn't it?"

After we made the baby, we sat facing each other on that huge bed, and Sammy cried. She didn't sob, or make any noises. She just sat there cross-legged, examining her fingers, silently popping out big fat tears. I saw them rolling down her cheeks.

"Why are you crying?" I asked, but I knew the answer. Because she was happy.

"Because I'm sad," said Sammy, still playing with her fingers.

"Sammy, you know something? You cry too much."

"Tough. If I'm sad, I'll cry."

"What the hell are you sad about?" I moaned.

"I'm sad because it's the end of an era."

"*What* era?"

"The end of being foot-loose and fancy-free," said Sammy. "Now we'll have to settle down and be more responsible. Now we'll be *truly* married, in every sense of the word. Marriage is children. All that stuff that comes *before* having children is semantics. That's living together, or shacking up, or going steady, or being pinned, or dating, or whatever, but having a baby is being married. Standing in front of an altar listening to a lot of gobbledegook about sickness and health, and until death do us part, doesn't make a couple married. If you don't have any children, you can break up any day in the week and never see each other again for the rest of your lives. But a kid keeps two people together *forever*, whether you get a divorce or not. We've been living together, Thomas. Now we're finally getting married."

Living together! Is *that* what we'd been doing, just *living* together? What the hell was Samantha talking about? Was she
unhappy with the thought of being *truly* married? Didn't she want
the child? I thought having a child was *her* idea.

"Don't you want to have a child?" I asked.

"Oh, come on, Thomas, don't be silly. Of *course* I want to have
our baby."

"Well, then are you unhappy about being *truly* married?"

"Thomas, that's the dumbest thing I ever heard."

"Then why are you so goddamn sad?"

"Because," she said, blowing her nose, "I'm sad, that's all.
Everybody has the right to be sad once in a while. Besides, time
is going by so fast. I think that's what's bothering me most of all.
We'll be grandparents before we know it."

"Well, you know what I say?"

"No," said Sammy. "What *do* you say?"

"I say that time flies when you're in good company." I grinned.

"Fine," said Sammy, lighting a cigarette.

"Listen, Sammy, like my grandmother used to say, you've got
two choices. You either grow old, or you don't."

Sammy smiled. "Bunch of real earthy philosophers in your
family, aren't there?"

Early in the morning I heard a bell toll the hour. I wasn't sure
if it had clanged four or five times.

"Thomas, are you up?"

"Yes."

"Thomas, we're broke!"

Sammy and I flew back to the States on New Year's Eve. We
celebrated twice, once by Paris time and once by New York
time.

We landed two minutes after midnight. It was depressing. Even
the customs inspector was blue. Terminals are not the place to
be on supposedly festive occasions.

We arrived at our apartment house just in time to see a drunk urinating on it. "Happy New Year," he said without looking up. "Happy New Year," replied Sammy cheerfully.

We didn't bother unpacking. I just turned out the lights and we climbed into bed. It was then that I felt the first sizable funk of the new year brewing in my bones.

"The apartment is musty and damp," I said darkly.

Sammy didn't answer.

"It's also gloomy and shitty," I added.

Sammy still didn't answer.

"Are you up?" I asked, knowing that she was.

"Yes."

"Aren't you interested in what I have to say?"

"No."

"Oh?" I said, feeling my funk turn quickly to anger.

"No, I'm not," continued Sammy, turning on her light and reaching for a cigarette. "I'm not because all you're doing is indulging yourself. You're tired from traveling, and customs, and lugging suitcases all over hell and back, and you're depressed. So you're doing what comes naturally. You're working yourself into a good juicy funk, and I won't be a part of it. Not unless you *really* want to worry about something."

"Like what?"

"Like what are we going to do for money tomorrow? We're broke, you know, or did you forget?"

"We're *that* broke?"

"Yes, we're that broke."

"Jesus," I said softly.

"Good night, Thomas."

"Good night," I said, feeling my anger turn quickly to fear.

Sammy put out her cigarette and turned off the light.

Christ, I thought, why the hell are we broke? How did Sammy let that happen to us? But it wasn't really Sammy's fault, was it? Wasn't I supposed to be the head of the household? Isn't that the man's job? Of course it is. Then how did I let such a thing

114

happen? What kind of man did Sammy marry? What must *she* be thinking right now? A light sweat was forming all over my body.

Sammy snapped her light on again and sat up. "Thomas, don't sweat it. I saved two thousand dollars! I took it out of our kitty and left it here in our savings account *before* we went to Europe."

She lit another cigarette.

"Thomas, learn to count your blessings. We had an unbelievably marvelous year in Europe, you finished your book, and we still have two thousand dollars in the bank to carry us until something happens. I love you, you love me, and we're going to have a baby. For Christ sake, what more can you ask? Just learn to count your blessings, son. You'll be much happier for it in the long run."

Sammy got up and went to the bathroom. She hollered out, "I'll bet you feel a hell of a lot better now, don't you? Didn't mean to play such a dirty trick on you, Tommy, but I had to get you out of that funk fast before you did us both in."

She came back to bed, said good night, and switched off her light. I watched her finish her cigarette, roll over, and go to sleep.

Smartass girl. What would I do without her?

"You know what, honey?" Sammy asked one morning just after breakfast.

"What?" I answered, never taking my eyes off the help wanted section of the *New York Times*.

"I saw a big black Carey Cadillac go by on Fifth Avenue yesterday. A very important businessman was sitting in the back."

"Fine," I said, turning the page.

"It was really fascinating."

"What was so fascinating?" I asked, circling a potential job with my pencil.

"The important businessman in the back. He was reading his *Wall Street Journal.*"

"What's so fascinating about that?"

"That's all he did. He just read his *Wall Street Journal.* The big black limousine stopped at the red light, and then moved on, and all that time all he did was read his goddamn *Wall Street Journal.*"

"How 'bout that," I muttered, disappointed at not finding any other opportunities on that page.

"That's unbelievable, isn't it? I mean, that's all the poor bastard did. Just read his paper. He never looked at all the people going by, or at the store windows, or anything. He just looked at his dull newspaper. What a shame." Sammy started gathering up the dishes. "Thomas."

"What?"

"Promise me you'll never sit in the back of a big black Carey Cadillac limousine with your nose stuck in a *Wall Street Journal,* never looking out of your window at the world going by. Do you promise?"

I promised. It seemed, that day, like a safe bet.

Being out of work with a pregnant wife can be a terrifying experience, but being out of work with a pregnant wife on a limited bank account that keeps dwindling each week can become unbelievably nerve-racking. Every unemployed day is a terrible defeat. You suffer the pangs of losing the battles, knowing full well the chances are good you'll lose the war, too. As the weeks slip by, your sense of inferiority grows. You slowly, at first, and then ever more quickly begin to adopt the personality of the defeatist: sensitive, moody, nervous, defensive, vulnerable.

Each job interview takes on a totally irrational importance in the overall scheme of things. The prospect of begging someone you loathe seeing for a function you would despise doing becomes your holy grail. Job interviews are all you talk about. You spend your waking hours trying to obtain them, researching them if you can, and hating them when they arrive. You dread it when you don't have any job interviews and you dread it when you do.

You begin to dread other things, too. You dread staying home and you dread going out. You dread finding yourself on the corner of Fifty-seventh Street and Madison Avenue at noon, dressed to the teeth in your best suit and tie, with no place to go. You dread browsing in an art gallery because if you enjoy yourself you'll feel guilty, and you dread going to an afternoon movie because you'll feel like a pervert when you come out. You dread bumping into friends and you *always* bump into enemies.

"Guess who I bumped into today?" I asked Sammy.

"Who?"

"Danny Cavaliere."

"Who's he?"

"He's an asshole."

"I thought you bumped into an asshole yesterday."

"I did," I said, slumping into my armchair. "That was another one."

"How come you keep bumping into assholes, Thomas?"

"Because I'm out of work, honey."

"What do you talk about when you bump into an asshole?" asked Sammy. She was ironing, and she was happy I was home so she could have someone to talk to.

"They ask me what I'm doing with myself and I tell them a lie."

"Why?"

"Because they would be delighted to know that I am out of work and I won't give them that satisfaction. So I lie."

Sammy lit a cigarette. "What kind of lies do you tell?"

"Good ones," I said, warming to the subject. "I told Cavaliere that my family bought a ranch in Colorado, just outside Denver, and that we moved there last year so that I could run it. I said that I was back in New York to attend a grain and feed convention. I told him that our ranch was a cattle ranch and that it was one of the biggest in the state.

"He asked me how many acres we had—which just happens to be a tough question—and I said one hundred acres, without

117

batting an eyelash. Then he asked me how many head of cattle we had—another toughie—and I said we had fifty thousand head."

"What did he say to that?" asked Sammy.

"He said he had worked on a cattle ranch in Texas for eight summers when he was going to high school and college, and if what I said was true, there wouldn't be enough room for the fifty thousand head of cattle on a hundred acres. He said the cattle would have to be stacked up, two or three on top of each other, and cattle don't graze that way."

"Then what happened?"

"Then he grinned at me and walked away, the damned asshole."

"Damned asshole," repeated Sammy, laughing.

Toward the end of April I decided to take stock of myself.

It had been one hell of a winter. The Great American Novel had been something short of a smashing success. Eight publishing companies had turned it down and a ninth was about to. My pile of rejection slips grew almost as fast as Sammy's stomach.

And my alternate plan of becoming president of a major corporation wasn't exactly steam-rolling along, either. I still hadn't found a job. I didn't even have an opportunity pending, and I was terrified to ask Sammy how much money we had left in the bank. My confidence and good cheer were dropping to an all-time low, and the cavalry was nowhere in sight.

What are you going to do? I asked myself.

Beats the shit out of me, I answered myself.

And so April became May.

When Sammy was four months pregnant, she looked eight months pregnant.

"I bought another maternity dress," she said apologetically. "I'm sorry but I really had to."

"What are you *sorry* about?" I asked, feeling a sudden fury in my system. "You only have two other maternity dresses and they're both falling apart."

"They are not."

"They are *so*. Come on, Sammy. I mean, I wouldn't call you an extravagant person who gets her kicks out of frittering away our hard-earned savings on jewels and furs and fancy clothes, now would I?"

"You have such a way with words," Sammy said admiringly.

"Sammy, be serious for a minute. I mean, it really burns me up when you have to say you're sorry because you bought one lousy maternity dress this month. What the hell are you so sorry about?"

I think I was trying to pick a fight.

"It's just that we can't afford it, Thomas. We can't, and my two other dresses are fine. But I just couldn't resist. The dress is so damn adorable. You'll see. I'll put it on for you."

When she left the room, I made myself a Scotch. We really couldn't afford that, either. I should be drinking beer, I thought.

My anger was subsiding. I was glad. I hated it when I became angry, and lately I was becoming angry more suddenly and more frequently than I ever had before.

Sammy came back into the living room. She was wearing her new dress, and it *was* adorable, just like she said. She flounced about the room, turning this way and that, smiling her huge smile because she felt pretty, and she was.

"That's another trait I hope our girl doesn't inherit from me," said Sammy.

"What trait's that?" I asked.

"My intolerably low will-power quotient. I get so mad at myself. It's a terrible feeling. The dress *is* absolutely adorable, though, isn't it, Thomas?"

"It looks fantastic."

Sammy flopped across the room, sat on my lap, and kissed me. "Do you *love* it? Not like it—*love* it?"

"I *love* it."

"I *knew* you would."

"Sammy, you just said we were going to have a girl. Are we?"

"Yes," she answered firmly, her arms around my neck, her big fat stomach under my hand.

"You're absolutely sure?"

"Absolutely."

"That's great!" I said, beaming. "I'm a lucky duck. One girl around the house is fine. Two girls around the house has to be better. It's only logical. Twice as many hugs and kisses, and things like that."

Sammy stood up. She smiled. "Just remember to spread 'em out nice and even, you old fart," and she walked out of the room.

Ever since she became pregnant, Sammy had begun walking differently. She seemed to assume a sort of majestic gait, her head and chin up, her backbone tucked in, her stomach way, way out. She was the kind of woman who carried her pregnancy well, thriving and flourishing on it. The more pregnant she got, the more she blossomed. The fatter her stomach, the prettier her face.

Sammy loved being pregnant. She enjoyed everything about it, and would have felt disappointed if she hadn't experienced every sensation, good *or* bad.

"Thomas, guess what?" she asked one morning before breakfast.

"What?"

"I just threw up!" she said happily. "Isn't that marvelous? I just threw up all over the place. I've got morning sickness! I really do!"

And then she kissed me on the mouth.

"Don't worry," she said, grinning. "I brushed my teeth."

Sammy became superstitious, too. She wasn't before she was pregnant, but she changed as soon as the doctor confirmed her "duck in the oven," as she liked to put it.

At first she simply avoided the old reliables—ladders, black cats, thirteens, hats on beds—and she refused to buy any baby furniture or baby clothes until the child was born.

But as time went on, her superstitions became far more unusual. She by-passed cripples, refusing to walk on the same side of the street if she saw one coming. She would not allow me to whistle in bed. She didn't bother to explain. She just asked me not to whistle in bed until the baby was born.

She began wearing certain clothes all the time, and not wearing other things ever again, claiming they were bad luck. She suddenly amassed a ton of good luck charms that she wore around her neck and wrists, and carried in her purse. She never went anywhere without them, and slept with some of the trinkets under the mattress on her side of the bed just about where her stomach was. Among the charms was a Catholic cross, a Jewish star, and half the saint medals that existed, including Saint Topaz, who wasn't really a saint at all.

"Why, Sammy?" I would ask occasionally.

"Why not?"

Eventually she made me warm my hands before I placed them on her stomach to feel the baby kick.

"Why, Sammy?"

"Because cold hands make a cold baby."

"How do you know?"

"I heard it."

"*Where'd* you hear it? Who told *that* one to you?"

"I just heard about it, that's all."

She didn't hear it. I'm sure she made it up. The problem was that she believed it.

One of the things that Sammy had looked forward to the most, about becoming pregnant, was the legitimate excuse to buy lots of maternity clothes. "I love them," she used to say. "They're so cute. I like them better than normal dresses sometimes, and nowadays you can buy maternity clothes for just about every occasion. They have evening dresses, slack outfits, sports clothes.

They even have bathing suits! Imagine, maternity bathing suits! I can't wait. I know I'm not going to have the will power at all when it comes to maternity clothes."

But she did have the will power.

She had to, and that's the thing that burned me up. By the time Sammy became pregnant, we were too poor to buy anything. The only daughter of John T. Wilkerson, president and chairman of the board of the American Steel Corporation, and she had to make do on three lousy maternity dresses. Absolutely absurd.

"It's absurd," I said, feeling the anger coming back.

"What's absurd?"

"That your family can run around buying race horses and yachts, but you have to make do on three lousy maternity dresses."

"Honey, please."

"It's goddamn absurd."

"Honey, we wouldn't want it any other way, would we?"

"You bet your ass we would. We're just too dumb to admit it," I said.

I was embarrassed. I put on a sweater and left the apartment. I guess I succeeded in taking all the fun out of Sammy's new maternity dress.

"Goddamnit, Tommy, shape up," said my sister.

"What have I done now, Geraldine?"

"It's what you *haven't* done," she said, lapping up the whipped cream on the top of her Irish coffee. We were sitting in Downey's again. It seems Geraldine and I were about to yell at each other. "You haven't found a job, that's what you haven't done. You're the darling of the unemployment line, Mr. Welfare of the Year, the sweetheart of—"

"Aw, cut it out."

"Cut what out? Christ, Tommy, how long can you go on counting rejection slips? So your book stinks. So what. At least you gave it a shot. Now face up to the facts of life and go to work."

"Where, Geraldine, my love? Where? It seems nobody wants a college dropout who got fired from a cuing machine company and wrote a lousy book."

"Really?" said my sister, signaling the waiter for another Irish coffee. "Who says you have to be a college dropout who got fired from a cuing machine company and wrote a lousy book? Personnel departments never check. For all they know you could have graduated second in your class at Harvard, and spent the last year of your life on a Rhodes scholarship at Cambridge."

"Jesus, Geraldine."

"Don't Jesus me, Tommy. Where's your nerve? Where's your guts? You sound like a wishy-washy piece of shit. And another thing . . ."

She paused just long enough for the waiter to put down her drink and take her old glass away.

"You'll need references."

"For what?"

"For whatever job you're applying for."

"How do I do that?" I asked, more in an effort to humor her than anything else.

"I'll tell you how, if you'll just shut up and listen. Where do you want to work?"

"I want a job as a guide at the National Broadcasting Company."

"Fine. So you go to the public library and look up the board of directors of NBC and pick a name. Look up the board of directors of a few other companies—you may want to use them, too—but use just one name from NBC. It's that simple, Tommy. How the hell do you think I got into Bryn Mawr?"

"You were a straight-A student, Geraldine."

"So were forty thousand other little girls in New York State alone. I went to the library and looked up the board of trustees of dear old Bryn Mawr, and used one of the names as a reference. That's how I got in."

"Geraldine," I said, bursting with pride and admiration, "you're fantastic."

"I'm also the only one with money, so I guess it's my check."

My sister dropped ten bucks on the table, kissed me, and split.

"I see by your form that you want to join our guide staff," said a squeaky-clean interviewer in the personnel department of the National Broadcasting Company.

"Yes, I do," I answered nervously.

"I also see by your form that you are a graduate of Harvard, and a Rhodes scholar."

"Yes, I am," I answered nervously.

The squeaky-clean interviewer tapped his pipe precisely three times in his ashtray and continued.

"I also see by your form that you have been referred to us by Mr. William Roger Webster."

"Yes, I have," I answered nervously.

"That's rather amazing," said the squeaky-clean gentleman behind the tidy brown desk.

"Amazing?" I asked nervously.

"Yes, amazing. Mr. Webster has been dead for three years."

"He has?"

"Been playing the old library gambit, haven't you?"

"I beg your pardon."

"The trouble with the books at the public library," said the interviewer, tapping his pipe precisely three times in his ashtray, "is that they're dated." He smiled and the interview was over.

I went home, turned on the television set, and planned how I would kill my sister. While I sat there, I thought of "The Cinderella Game."

Sammy and I were having tea in the courtyard of the Museum of Modern Art.

"Sammy, dear," I said lovingly, "why did you marry me?"

"What's up, Thomas?" asked Sammy.

"Nothing's up, honey. I'm just curious why a nice girl like you would marry a bum like me."

"Because you're great in bed," she answered, and took a sip of tea.

"Just because I'm great in bed?"

"Isn't that enough?"

"I was hoping there was more than just one reason."

"Well," said Sammy, "you wear funny hats, and your hair looks like Brillo in the morning, and—"

"Aw, be serious for a minute."

"Okay. I'd say, then, that the real reason I married you was because you enjoy life, you're always nice to me, you always find time to do sweet things, and you never beat me up."

"But didn't you really marry me for my money?" I asked, biting into a doughnut. "I mean, wasn't I going to be a big success and all that? Wasn't *that* the real reason you married me?"

"Not at all. I never cared if you were a big success or not and still don't. Just as long as you were happy and we were together."

"You'll say anything just to get me in bed with you."

"True."

"All right, Mrs. Christian, now comes the big question." I straightened up in my chair and let it fly. "How long do we have until we're wiped out? I mean, how long will it be until there's absolutely no money left in the bank?"

"Another month," said Sammy, taking a sip of tea.

"Another month!" I repeated, suddenly horrified. And then, with as much bravado as I could muster, I added, "Well, don't you worry, Mrs. Christian. I don't want you to worry about that."

"I'm *not* worried," Sammy said.

"You're not?"

"Nope."

"How come?"

"Because you'll think of something," she answered, and wiped her mouth with her napkin.

"I already have," I said, and beamed.

"You have? Great! You want to tell me about it?"

"Yes." And that's when I told Sammy about "The Cinderella Game."

"Geraldine, lend me twenty thousand dollars."

I caught her just as she was about to lick the whipped cream off the top of her Irish coffee. Her tongue froze.

"Huh?" she said. She was obviously stunned. In retrospect, I shall always remember that moment as the only time I ever made my sister Geraldine speechless.

"Huh?" she repeated.

"Geraldine, lend me twenty thousand dollars. If you do, I'll double it for you in a year."

"Waiter!" howled Geraldine, gnawing on the nail of her right index finger. It was easy to see that Geraldine had become instantly disturbed. She always bit the nail of her right index finger when she was disturbed.

When our waiter arrived, she asked for another Irish coffee. *"Make that a double!"* she boomed, causing a quartet in the next booth to turn and look at her.

I remained calm.

After all, she was my younger sister, wasn't she? I mean, it's not the manliest thing in the world to be afraid of your younger sister, is it?

"I'm not afraid of you, Geraldine."

"What?"

"Nothing."

The waiter came back with Geraldine's Irish coffee.

"Did you *really* ask me to loan you twenty thousand dollars?" she asked.

The waiter exchanged the full glass for the empty one and quickly walked away.

"Yes."

"Why?" snapped Geraldine.

"I need it. I want to develop an idea for a television show I thought up. It's a great idea, Geraldine."

Geraldine slid down into her seat and jammed her hands into the pockets of her raincoat. She was frowning from ear to ear.

"Geraldine, listen to me for once in your life. For the last six months I've been home a lot. Too much. All I did—when I wasn't looking for a job—was watch TV. I watched daytime television until it was coming out of my ears. Have you ever watched daytime television?"

I didn't wait for an answer.

"It's garbage, Geraldine. It's the most asinine, banal, mind-blowing rot you've ever seen in your life, and I—your beloved brother—have just thought of the asininest, banalest, mind-blowingest show of them all. Geraldine, I've got a daytime television idea that every housewife and unemployed husband in America is just going to suck right up. It's the most commercial, exciting, identifiable—"

"You *did* say twenty thousand dollars, didn't you?"

"Geraldine, I'm almost broke. We've got about another month left before they cart Sammy and me to debtors' prison. I need money to live on while I try and sell my show idea, and if worst comes to worst . . ."

I stopped talking in midsentence. The thought of what would happen if worst came to worst was too horrendous to verbalize.

"What will happen if worst comes to worst?" asked Geraldine.

"Nothing," I said, getting off the subject. "Geraldine, I know I'm asking for a lot, but don't give me your famous third degree, or that goddamn frown. Either loan me the money or *don't* loan me the money. But don't give me—"

"Shut up, Tommy. Just shut the hell up."

I shut up.

"You know, Tommy," said Geraldine, sitting bolt upright in her chair, "I'll bet you think I have twenty thousand dollars tucked away in my stocking drawer, or maybe under my pillow. Am I right? Am I, Tommy?"

"Aw, get off it, Geraldine." She was really making me mad.

"Twenty bucks I have in my stocking drawer. Twenty thousand I don't. *Waiter!*"

The waiter ran over.

"Can I have my goddamn check, please?" Geraldine asked for it as though she had been waiting for hours.

The check was there in a matter of seconds.

Geraldine stuffed it in her pocket and slid out of her seat. She was halfway down the bar when she turned and yelled, "I'll send you the money in the morning. If you piss it away, I'll kick your ass from one end of Fifth Avenue to the other." She didn't wait for me to thank her.

It was my turn to be stunned.

I just sat there and stared at the seat she had just left. And then I heard the lilting melody of her truck driver voice. She had returned and was standing in Downey's doorway.

"What's the name of this epic television idea of yours?" she roared.

" 'The Cinderella Game.' "

"You know what, Tommy?"

"What?"

"I like it." Geraldine smiled and disappeared.

"So that's your idea?" said the network television executive. I tried to detect an inflection in his voice that might give me a clue to his feelings, but there wasn't much chance for inflection in "So that's your idea?"

"Yes," I said with authority.

"Hmmmm," he said, and got up. I spent the next three or four minutes watching the network executive pace back and forth behind his desk. His name was David Greenburg, he wore a pin-striped suit, a blue oxford shirt, a sincere tie, and he was about my age. How did he become so important at such an early age?

"I like it," he said, finally.

That's how he became so important.

"But," he continued, "I'm not sure I like your idea enough to spend forty or fifty thousand dollars on it to make a pilot."

My stomach fell into my groin.

"About how much, do you estimate, would it cost to do a pilot tape of your idea?" asked Mr. Greenburg.

"About forty thousand," I said firmly, choosing the lower of the two figures Mr. Greenburg had mentioned, since I hadn't the slightest idea what a pilot tape would cost.

"Hmmmm," he said again, and sat down behind his desk. The network executive arranged some papers in a neat pile, swiveled his large padded chair around so that he was looking out over Manhattan, and continued. "We have a few problems," he said, staring at the Hudson River. "For one thing, I've spent just about all my development money for the year. For another, you're not an experienced producer. I don't know whether you can make this idea of yours work."

"I'll make it work. I guarantee you I'll make it work."

David Greenburg, network executive, swiveled himself back to me and said, "I'll think about it. Call me in a week."

Mr. Greenburg thanked me for coming, shook my hand, and walked me to his door. Mr. Greenburg's secretary smiled and asked me if I could find my way to the elevators. I told her that I could, and immediately got lost. After a few minutes I found myself walking down a corridor that led back to Mr. Greenburg's office. When I arrived there, Mr. Greenburg's secretary asked if I had forgotten something.

"Yes," I said, and proceeded to make the boldest move I would ever make in my entire life.

"I would like to see Mr. Greenburg again," I said. "There's one other thing I want to tell him."

"What did you say?" asked Sammy, checking the roast that was browning in the oven.

"I told him that I believed in 'The Cinderella Game' so much, I wasn't afraid to put my money where my mouth was."

"Bravo," said Sammy, jabbing the meat with a large fork.

"I said that I would put up half the money to make the pilot if the American Broadcasting Company would put up the other half."

"Wonderful," said my wife. "How much money would you have to put up, Thomas?"

"Twenty thousand dollars."

Sammy dropped her fork.

"Say that again, Thomas."

I said it again.

"You mean," said Sammy, sitting down, "that you put up twenty thousand dollars and the American Broadcasting Company puts up twenty thousand dollars, and you make a pilot of 'The Cinderella Game'? Is that right?"

"That's right."

"Then what happens?"

"Then the network executives evaluate the show and decide whether or not to put it on the air. If it goes on the air, we're rich."

"And if it doesn't?" asked Sammy.

"We lose our twenty thousand dollars."

"*What* twenty thousand dollars?"

"I asked Geraldine to lend me twenty thousand dollars. She sent me a check yesterday."

Sammy sat staring at her clasped hands. After a minute or two she looked up and asked, "What did the man say, Thomas?"

"He said, 'Tommy, you have yourself a deal!' "

And then Sammy's water bag broke.

I met Gil Mack in front of Saint Patrick's Cathedral. We went inside and took the last row on the right.

"How's your daughter?" whispered Gil.

"Very small," I whispered. "Gil, I need a lawyer."

"What have you done now?"

"I'm not sure," I said, and instantly felt panic-stricken.

"You look pale, Tommy."

"I feel pale."

"Okay, tell me all about it."

I told him all about it.

"Jesus Christ," whispered Gil Mack appropriately.

"Shhhh," said a Catholic several rows in front of us.

Gil Mack crossed himself and the two of us bowed our heads.
The Catholic returned to his prayers.

"You know something, Tommy?"

"What?"

"I can see why Sammy's water bag broke."

"Good for you."

"You know something else?" whispered Gil.

"What?"

"You need a good lawyer."

"That's what I said twenty minutes ago."

"And I've got just the man. He's a friend of my father's and
he's fantastic. I guess he's in his late fifties. He looks like Humphrey Bogart and talks like Humphrey Bogart. He went to City
College night school with my father. During the day I think he
was a hood. My father told me that after he graduated night
school, he disappeared off the face of the earth. When he reap-
peared, he was a millionaire. He owned a chain of motion picture
theaters, a stable of horses, and a client list that included some
of the biggest movie and television stars in the country. He knows
all the tricks of the trade, and he's one of the toughest negotiators
in the business. At least that's what my father says."

"What's his name?"

"And another thing," said Gil. "He won't take you if he doesn't
like you, and it doesn't matter if you have all the money in the
world, or if you're as poor as a church mouse."

"Who is he?"

"I met him once, and I can tell you this: If you're honest with him, you're okay. But if you try and con him, you're dead."

"Con who, Gil?"

"I'll have my father call him today and set up an appointment for you."

"Goddamnit, Gil, what the hell's his name?"

"Paul Blum."

Paul Blum looked and talked exactly like Humphrey Bogart.

"If what you say is true," he said, with a lisp out of the corner of his mouth, "then I've got to hand it to you. You've got guts."

I smiled.

"Either that," continued Paul Blum, "or you're the world's biggest shmuck."

I stopped smiling.

But I wasn't sure if I should get mad or not.

Paul Blum's guys-and-dolls approach bemused me. I never knew when he was serious and when he wasn't. He had just called me a shmuck, yet it sounded nice. And his warm smile and twinkly eyes seemed anything but hostile. I think he was enjoying me.

"So what are you, a guy with guts or a shmuck?"

I scratched my head and thought about that, and then I said, "Mr. Blum, I think I'm a little of both."

"And then what did he say?" asked Sammy, stirring a vat of vegetable soup.

"He said he liked me because I was ambitious, honest, enthusiastic, and terribly in need of help."

"Amen," moaned my Sammy.

"And then he told me what his services would cost."

"Shall I drop my spoon now or wait until you're finished?"

"Might as well drop it now."

"Why?"

"Because he gets half of my profits from the show if it goes on television . . . or anywhere else, for that matter."

"What *could* be the profits of your show?" asked Sammy.

"Between two and four thousand dollars a week, depending on how good a deal Paul negotiates."

"So at worst, you would get a thousand dollars a week and Paul would get a thousand dollars a week."

"That's correct."

"That's not correct. That's *fantastic!*" said Sammy, stirring her vat again. "You know what Sugar Ray Robinson used to say, don't you?"

"No," I said, sighing heavily. "What *did* Sugar Ray Robinson used to say?"

"He said fifty percent of somethin' is better than a hundred percent of nothin'."

"Good old Sugar sure was smart."

"Let's hope Paul Blum is, too," said Sammy, kissing the end of my nose.

Paul Blum was more than smart.

He was godlike.

First of all, he helped me put together a staff of experienced television production people, which immediately dispelled the American Broadcasting Company's notion that I might not be able to produce the program.

Next, he drew up a budget that was ten thousand dollars more than I had estimated, and then verified the entire fifty thousand dollars to Mr. Greenburg and his entourage of business affairs experts and lawyers.

And finally, he negotiated a deal that was unbelievably good. I got fifty percent of the foreign rights, fifty percent of the merchandising rights, and a weekly profit of five thousand dollars.

"Paul, you were great!" I roared as soon as the two of us walked out of the American Broadcasting Company building.

"I know," he said.

"Five thousand dollars a week! I don't believe it."

"Remember, half of that's mine," said Paul, smiling.

"Gladly," I said, giving him a big bear hug. "I'm sure you know what Sugar Ray Robinson used to say."

"No," said Paul Blum, "and I don't *care* what Sugar Ray Robinson used to say. All I care about is that you make that pilot work so that those network geniuses up there put it on the air."

"I'll make it work," I said, feeling the old ton of panic sliding back on my shoulders. But I was excited, too. For the first time I felt I had a fighting chance.

"Dear God," I said in the Central Synagogue, on the corner of Lexington Avenue and Fifty-fifth Street, "please make it work. Please make my program a smash hit and a huge financial success. Let 'The Cinderella Game' become the number one daytime television show in America, and let my Sammy and me become fantastically wealthy."

I paused for a second to catch my breath.

"And, dear God, please forgive me if I sound materialistic, and grasping, and avaricious, and greedy, and money-oriented, and all that stuff. I'm sorry. I really am, but that's what makes me happy, and if You don't know that by now, then You're doing a slipshod job up there."

I stopped. My speech to God in this place wasn't going as well as my speech in Saint Patrick's. When I talked to God there, the plea rolled out just the way I wanted it to. Maybe that's because there were other people in Saint Pat's. There wasn't a soul in Central Synagogue. Just a cleaning woman vacuuming the altar. Every now and then she looked at me, and I was certain she knew I was an atheist.

"Dear God, I might have been an atheist before, and I *still* might have a little atheism in me, but I'm trying. I've been to Saint Patrick's. I'm here. I'm trying to go everywhere You are so that I can talk to You."

I suddenly wondered if I should have a hat on. I remembered that Jewish men wore hats in their houses of worship.

"Dear God, I'm sorry I'm not wearing a hat. The reason I'm not wearing a hat is because I don't own a hat. But I'll get one. I'll have one the next time."

And then I quit.

This was all a waste of time.

Not only was it a waste of time, but it was childish and immature. Wandering around the city going into every church and synagogue I could find was stupid.

Or was it?

What if there really was a God?

But wasn't God for big things like sickness and death?

Maybe. But maybe He was for little things like success and wealth, too.

What the hell. What did I have to lose?

"Dear God, we do the pilot of my idea tomorrow. I've worked like a dog for the last six weeks on this show of mine. I've worked seven days a week, sometimes twenty hours a day. I've checked and double-checked everything over and over again. I'll go back and check everything one more time tonight, and then we'll do the pilot tomorrow afternoon. And then it's in Your hands.

"Tell You what I'll do, God. I'll believe in You for the rest of my life, no matter what happens to the program. How's that? It'll just be a hell of a lot easier to believe in You if the program's a success. Please, dear God, think it over and see what You can do."

He thought it over all right.

Three weeks later, Sammy said that David Greenburg had called while I was out, and wanted me to call him back as soon as I got in.

When I called Mr. Greenburg's office, his secretary asked if I could drop by that afternoon at four o'clock.

I hugged Sammy and said, "This is it! He's going to tell me it's on the air. I know it. I just know it."

That was true. I *did* know it. Our pilot was terrific. The show worked like a charm. The studio audience loved it and I was certain the network executives liked it, too.

At four o'clock I was sitting in front of David Greenburg's desk.

"Tommy," said Mr. Greenburg, "we're not going to schedule 'The Cinderella Game.' The show was good. In fact, it was *very* good. But we're just not going to make any changes for the time being. I'm sorry, Tommy. I know how hard you worked on the pilot."

I guess I never really expected God to do anything. I never gave Him any reason to do anything for me in the past. Why should He do anything for me now?

Helplessness is such a rotten feeling. There's nothing you can do about it.

Being helpless is like being paralyzed. It's a sickness. The cure calls for a monumental effort to stand up and start walking somewhere, anywhere. But that takes some doing. David Greenburg had infected me with a monumental case of helplessness, and I couldn't stand up. I just lay on our living room couch, lethargic and inert, staring out of our window at the building across the street. Sometimes I wondered if there was another desolate soul in the apartment opposite mine, staring at my window.

Sammy felt helpless, too. I could tell. She didn't know how to comfort me. I knew she was in pain, but I didn't care. Not caring is symptomatic of the disease.

Geraldine came to the apartment and tried her rough-and-tumble form of medicine.

"I'm not worried about the money," she said bravely, "so don't *you* worry about it."

"Okay," I said, looking out the window, too helpless to comprehend responsibility.

136

Geraldine came over to the couch, pushed my feet aside, sat down, and said, "The money doesn't bother me, Tommy. What *does* bother me is this boring prima donna act you've been performing for the last—"

"Go away, Geraldine."

She went away.

And that's the way it was for fourteen days and fifteen nights. On the morning of the fifteenth day, Sammy sat down beside me and said, "Thomas, we have seventy-two dollars in the bank."

"Okay," I said, looking out of the window, too helpless to comprehend terror.

I stayed on the couch that entire day and that entire night, and when I awoke the next morning, nothing had changed.

"Thanks a lot, God," I said. "Thanks a goddamn lot." And then I rolled over on my side and stared at a purple pillow.

The next day was my birthday.

I celebrated by sitting in the bathtub contemplating my toes and my future.

Geraldine's husband had offered me some nebulous sort of job in one of his plants near Bridgeport. There must have been some pretty good discussions over *that* one, I thought to myself, noticing for the first time that the nails on my little toes had all but disappeared.

My sister must have *really* jammed me down poor old Harrison's throat.

"But I don't need him," H.T. must have said.

"But he's my brother," Geraldine must have said.

"But I don't *need* him, Gerry."

"But he's my *brother!*"

"Okay, I need him. I need him!"

Poor bastard. Anyway, Harrison only has himself to blame. He wanted Geraldine. He got Geraldine. Like my grandmother used to say, if you get them, you deserve it.

I guess that's neither here nor there. The point was, should I move to Bridgeport, Connecticut, and do some crummy job in one of my brother-in-law's factories, a vague and ill-defined job that my brother-in-law concocted to shut up his nagging wife?

No.

But did I have a choice?

No.

So there it is, folks. There the hell it is.

And it's my birthday today, folks. Twenty-eight going on thirty. Happy goddamn birthday, Tommy.

"Thomas," Sammy called. "You're wanted on the telephone."

"Who is it?"

"David Greenburg."

I came to the phone sopping wet. A small puddle of bath water began forming at my feet. Sammy said something about drying off or I would get electrocuted. I grabbed the receiver.

"Hello," I said.

"Hello, Tommy, this is David. David Greenburg."

"Hi ya, David," I said, looking at Sammy.

And then David Greenburg said two simple sentences. They were, "There's been a change in plans. We're putting 'The Cinderella Game' on the air."

Sammy knew exactly what David Greenburg said. I knew by the expression on her face. Her eyes were filling up with tears, and she just stood there with the baby in her arms, smiling and crying.

David Greenburg spoke about coming to his office to discuss studio facilities and press releases, but Sammy and I were kissing and hugging, and it was difficult for me to concentrate on David Greenburg, and studio facilities, and press releases.

"Hello," said David Greenburg. "Are you there?"

"Yes, I'm here," I said, "but you're going to have to excuse me, David. I think I'm going to throw up."

And I did, just making it to the bathroom in time.

That afternoon I went to the bank and withdrew the remnants of our savings account. It came to exactly seventy-two dollars and thirty-three cents. I left a dollar in the account so that we wouldn't have to close it, and used the rest to celebrate.

We had drinks at Toots Shor's and dinner at "21." We were so excited, Sammy didn't even complain, but we *did* have to watch the menu carefully. I kept score with a pencil and paper.

We started by including tips for the hatcheck girl and the doorman, and a cigar for myself. We even included the cost of a taxi back to our apartment. Then we began deciding what to eat. The magic number, less tips, taxi, cigar, and baby-sitter, was sixty-two dollars. Whenever we went over that total, we went back and juggled the entrées. We ended up with roast chicken and chopped sirloin, which we divided between us. I was allowed one Scotch, and we split a small bottle of the cheapest wine, which wasn't so cheap. The waiters, particularly the headwaiter, hated us the moment they saw us, and we didn't let them down.

That night we sat on the couch and reminisced while I finished our last bottle of Scotch. For the first time in our marriage I confessed that I had run off to Martha's Vineyard with Mike Malloy and Gil Mack the weekend before our wedding.

"I knew you'd run somewhere," Sammy said, "but I knew you'd come back."

We talked about the snake in Vancouver, and the disastrous dinner at Ernie's in San Francisco, and my ill-fated "system" for selling Transamerican cuing machines.

"I thought it was a great system," said Sammy. "I remember you saying, 'Think of all the flowers we'll get to smell and the meadows we'll be able to lie in,' and you were right. It was just wonderful."

I thought about Sammy going limp and falling through my arms in a dead faint in Dallas, and the time we were in Las Vegas and I got the cable from the Transamerica Cuing Machine Company that "terminated our relationship."

Sammy giggled. "You just finished telling me, the day before, that we had nothing to worry about."

We talked about Mike Malloy, our flat in London, and Sammy's first taste of bitters.

"You called it stale, warm beer," I recalled, wheezing with laughter. It was late and I was drunk. Everything struck me funny, the couch was extra-comfortable, and Sammy looked prettier than she had ever looked in her life. It was a delicious night.

We talked about the rain in Nice, and the rain in Saint Tropez. "Remember our first night in Saint Tropez?" asked Sammy. "We ate at the Entrée restaurant, and you thought all the men wanted to rape me!"

We talked and talked and talked, and at one point, in the wee hours of the morning, Sammy put me to bed.

"And you did it all by yourself," she said. "Nobody helped you. No Wilkersons, no Christians, nobody. Just you, yourself. Happy birthday, Thomas."

But I didn't hear her.

I had fallen asleep content with the dream that someday soon millions of people, coast to coast, would be watching "The Cinderella Game," a Thomas Christian Production in association with the American Broadcasting Company. I couldn't possibly have dreamed, that night, what an unbelievable phenomenon my television program would become.

I never dreamed that within six months, "The Cinderella Game" would be a smashing success on both daytime *and* nighttime television, and that within a year "The Cinderella Game" would be a national slogan.

"The Cinderella Game," the television game show that allowed contestants to win prizes simply by wishing for them. Sickness, disease, and personal problems were not a prerequisite for appearing on the program. Being at the right place, at the right time, was. You just had to be singled out by a pretty blond "Cinderella" girl, and tell her your wish. It was that easy.

But finding a "Cinderella" girl wasn't that easy. They were never where you thought they would be, and always where you least expected them. One might be sitting next to you on the eight-fourteen commuter train into Atlanta, or be concealed underneath a Santa Claus costume on Fifth Avenue.

Sometimes the "Cinderella" girl granted your wish and sometimes she didn't, but if she did, you would be flown to New York for an all-expenses-paid weekend and an appearance on the television show. There, in front of a studio audience of five hundred people and a national audience of over twenty million Americans, the program would make your dream come true.

Often the wishes the show granted were ordinary and relatively insignificant: a color television set, a new wardrobe, a trip to Hawaii. Other times they were startling: a forty-foot yacht for a young Seattle family of six, a three-month trip around the world for a retired couple from Chicago, a Rolls-Royce for a New York cab driver.

In the years ahead, "The Cinderella Game" would make a lot of people happy, and it would make me rich.

David Greenburg had become my fairy prince. By waving his magic network wand, he transformed me from an unemployed bum with seventy-two dollars and thirty-three cents in the bank, into a respected television producer earning close to three thousand dollars a week, with the opportunity to become richer and more respected.

The rich get richer, so they say.

And it's true. They do.

Within six months, I would repay my sister her twenty thousand dollars, plus the additional twenty thousand dollars I had promised her, and I would have a second game show on national television, earning me another three thousand dollars a week.

By the end of the year, Sammy and I would move from our shithouse walk-up into a fashionable three-bedroom apartment in the East Seventies. The move made Sammy sad. "I'm going to miss that place," she said as we drove away. "It was full of love and good times and sentimental goodies." Then she added with irritation, "The goddamn Seventies don't impress *me.*" I remember that her remarks annoyed me, but that the annoyance would quickly pass. In those days there wasn't time to be annoyed.

With the start of the new year I would have my third television program on the air, and before that year was over I would have my fourth. Two of the four programs would be seen both day and night, and I would be called the King of the Game Shows.

King of the Game Shows.

And the King would be making over twenty thousand dollars a week, just two years from the night he had seventy-two dollars and thirty-three cents to his name.

Within three years from this very night—the night that Samantha Jane Wilkerson Christian tucked her relieved and happy drunk into bed—I would be a millionaire, with enough money in the bank to retire. I could spend the rest of my life never going to work again; just waking up in the morning and going to bed at night, with plenty of time to smell flowers and lie in meadows and make abortive attempts to write the Great American Novel.

Perhaps that's what I should have done, but I didn't.

I couldn't.

Too many things would happen too fast.

Life would become like *Alice in Wonderland.*

Dozens of lawyers and financial advisers would appear and help me build a moneymaking empire that would include over a dozen companies, all under the corporate banner of Thomas Christian Enterprises. Who would have thought that night, in our little shithouse apartment at Fortieth Street and Third Avenue, that I would eventually become president of a company and chairman of a board of directors? Who would have imagined that I would be able to address an annual stockholders meeting and discuss financial conditions, acquisition, sales problems, and future trends so well that everyone would leave the auditorium pleased that his stock was in my hands?

And they would be right. My company would have a Midas touch.

In the years ahead, Thomas Christian Enterprises would own a chain of Steak House Restaurants in the ten top resort areas in the country, a major league hockey team, and a tremendously profitable Broadway show. We would control a motion picture about to begin shooting in Spain, an industrial-film business in New York, an oil-drilling-equipment company in El Paso, Texas, and a high-class chain of hot dog stands in London, Paris, and Rome called the American Meat Machine.

The American Meat Machine.

The rich get richer.

Who would have dreamed, that night, that Sammy and I would never have to wash another dish if we didn't want to, or dirty underwear, or the kitchen floor? Somebody would always be there to do it for us.

Who would have dreamed that we would never have to stand in line at a bank, or a supermarket, or a box office? We would never have to keep a bank balance, or know when the rent was due, or how much our insurance premiums were. Someone would do it for us. Someone would make our appointments, wash our cars, cut our lawns, buy our anniversary presents, and send out our Christmas cards, get-well telegrams, and sympathy notes. Someone would sweep our floors, dust our lamps, and make our beds.

We would never have to take a bus or a taxi, if we didn't want to, because someone would always be there to pick us up and deliver us. We would never have to refill our refrigerators, or our liquor cabinets, or our ice cube trays.

We would never have to look at the prices on clothes or cars or menus again.

Who could have dreamed *those* kind of dreams the night Sammy tucked me into bed? That night, it was just nice to know we wouldn't starve next week, or that I wouldn't have to work for my brother-in-law in Bridgeport, Connecticut.

"And you did it all by yourself," Sammy had said. "Nobody helped you. No Wilkersons, no Christians, nobody. Just you, yourself. Happy birthday, Thomas."

But I didn't hear her.

If I had, I would have said, *"We* did it, Sammy. We did it together. It was always you and me, babe."

Sometimes I think back to that night and wonder what I would have done differently if I had it to do all over again. I think of things I should have done, and things I could have done.

Shoulda, woulda, coulda, like my sister used to say.

Part 3

*T*hree years had passed and Sammy and I were in London. It was snowing, but our suite in the Dorchester Hotel was warm and cozy. Sammy was sitting in a large, ornate armchair that had an exceptionally high back. She was dressed more exquisitely than I had seen her dressed in a long time. She was wearing a white evening gown that clung to her like a piece of elastic. I could see the outline of her ribs and hipbones, yet the dress was in good taste.

I was in my tuxedo.

Our chauffeur was waiting downstairs in the new Rolls-Royce I had bought earlier that day. Sammy and I were going to the premiere of a motion picture my company had financed. I rationalized buying the Rolls-Royce to celebrate the premiere. I planned to ship the car to New York as soon as the London trip was over.

Our maid came into the room with our drinks.

I felt good.

I liked everything about our life.

Sammy took her drink from the tray and smiled one of her forced smiles at the maid. I knew the smile well. I wondered if the maid knew it wasn't a smile at all. I took my drink and the maid left the room.

Sammy looked at me and said, "Thomas, dear, it's such a

waste, and it's not as much fun. It really isn't. We don't need to hire a chauffeur and a maid when we travel, and we don't need this gigantic suite. Any room in the Dorchester is nice enough. You can stop trying to impress me. God knows I'm impressed. I loved you, honey, when we lived in our dear old shithouse walk-up. If I loved you there, I sure as hell can love you in a forty-five-dollar-a-day room. I don't need a suite. Just because we have a lot of money doesn't mean we have to spend it like there was no tomorrow."

"Sammy, relax. It's all Alice in Wonderland."

"Thomas, I can't relax knowing we're paying a chauffeur all that money just to sit outside and wait to take us around the corner, or a maid who does nothing but loiter in the kitchen waiting to serve us drinks."

Sammy came over and sat down beside me on the couch.

"Thomas, dear, no matter what you do, someone else is going to do it a little better. Remember the time we chartered the plane to take us to Saint Moritz to go skating? You thought that was pretty snazzy until you saw that Greek shipbuilder, whatever his name was, being chauffeured from the bottom of the mountain to the top in his private helicopter, so he didn't have to bother with the ski lifts. Somebody's always going to do it better than you, honey, so why not get out of the race and enjoy yourself?"

"Are you all finished, Samantha?"

"Yes, I'm finished."

"Then let's go."

"I hope you didn't forget that it's your anniversary tomorrow," said my secretary politely.

"Oh, my God, I did!"

"I thought you might," she continued politely, "so I bought two or three things. You can look at them and take your choice."

She showed me a gorgeous pair of leather boots, an elegant bed jacket with collar and cuffs crocheted in French lace, and a small fur coat.

"It's called a fun fur," said my secretary politely. "They're *the* thing to wear now. I've seen them in *Vogue* and *Harper's* lately, and the coat isn't really that expensive. I personally think your wife would look great in the fur coat. You can save the other presents for her birthday and for Valentine's Day, if you want to."

"Okay, let's do that," I said.

"By the way," said my secretary politely, "the store is the Nic-Nac, on Madison Avenue near Sixty-second Street. The salesgirl I bought the coat from is named Betty. I told her that if anyone asked, *you* bought it from her, and I described you to her. She's short, she has red hair, she's cute and very nice. The Nic-Nac, on Madison Avenue near Sixty-second Street. The salesgirl is Betty."

I thanked my secretary. "I appreciate your efficiency, Sally, only next time remind me far enough ahead so that I can buy the present myself."

My secretary smiled politely, and said she would.

I gave the fur coat to Sammy the next day. She was delighted with it and complimented me on my good taste.

"Happy birthday to you. Happy birthday to you. Happy birthday, dear Caroline. Happy birthday to you."

"Where are you, Daddy?"

"I'm in Los Angeles, California, sweetheart." The telephone connection was terrible. "Can you hear me, Carrie?"

"Yes."

"Happy birthday, honey."

"When are you coming home?"

"Soon," I lied.

"Good."

"How was the party, sweetheart?"

"Fine."

"That's good."

"Daddy, why did you have to go there on my birthday?"

"I had an important business meeting," I answered, wondering if I sounded as silly and as guilty as I felt, and if a four-year-old could detect that sort of thing. "Carrie," I said quickly, "did all your friends come?"

"Yes."

"Good. Did you like the present your mother and I bought you?" I didn't know what Sammy got her. She should have told me.

"Yes."

"That's nice."

"Daddy, when did you say you were coming home?"

"Soon. Carrie, who's my favorite little girl in the whole world?"

"I am."

"And who's going to grow up and be my best friend?"

"I am."

"I've got to run, sweetheart. Give me a big kiss and a big hug."

She gave me a big kiss and a big hug.

"Good-bye, sweetheart."

"Good-bye, Daddy."

I hung up the phone and felt lousy.

"I felt lousy, Paul, and I couldn't figure out why."

Paul Blum and I were having a corned beef and cole slaw on rye, with Russian dressing, in the Sixth Avenue Delicatessen. The Sixth Avenue Delicatessen was our summer White House. Paul and I made most of our important decisions there, decisions concerning life and love, what football games to bet on, and what we would do with ourselves when the merry-go-round came to a grinding halt.

Paul Blum laughed.

"What's a nice gentile boy like you doing with the Jewish Guilt Syndrome?" he asked. "You've heard of the Jewish Guilt Syndrome, haven't you? That's the gridge you get in the pit of your stomach when a business partner calls you at home on a Sunday and you're embarrassed that you're not at the office. It's the same

150

gridge you get when your kid cries on a long-distance phone call. If you've got the Jewish Guilt Syndrome, you're a goner. That's why gentiles live longer than Jews. They rarely get the disease. You must have caught it from me."

Paul Blum took a massive bite of his sandwich and continued. A piece of cole slaw hung from his lower lip.

"My mother used to tell me a story about a Jewish boy who fell in love with a beautiful gentile girl. When he asked the girl how he could prove his love to her, she told him to cut out his mother's heart and bring it to her. So the son ran home and cut out his mother's heart. On the way back, he tripped and fell and dropped the heart, and the heart said, 'Did you hurt yourself, my son?' That story has destroyed more Jewish males than Hitler."

"Did it destroy you?" I asked.

"No."

"How come?"

"Because in the middle of the story, I kicked my mother in the ass and left home."

Somehow Paul Blum always seemed to put everything in its proper perspective.

"Thomas, can you please leave your work and your staff at the office? Can't you try to maintain some semblance of privacy, a private life, a home life of some sort? Can't you try for my sake?"

I looked into my glass and saw that the ice cubes had diluted the Grand Marnier, so that now its color was a sickish yellow. Why were we discussing this tired point again? Lately, we always seemed to be discussing this tired point.

"Sammy," I said with a sigh, "the fellows won't stay long, and it's the best time to do this. The meeting's early tomorrow morning and I've got to be briefed on the details. I don't want to blow this one."

"But that's what you have an office for," said Sammy, standing up and moving to a chair closer to me. "This is your *home*. It's

151

where you relax and talk and play with your child and hold me in your arms. It's where you invite *other* friends over for dinner, friends who aren't in the business. Doctors, lawyers, Indian chiefs, people other than your financial advisers, your lieutenants, your secretarial staff, your negotiators. Your home is *not* an extension of your office, or a change of scenery for Paul, and Seymour, and David, and Walt, and your secretary, and God knows who else."

I got up and went to the bar. I plopped another ice cube into my Grand Marnier and stood there twirling it around in the glass with my finger. My back was to Sammy, and I spoke looking into my drink.

"Sammy, I'm beginning to get the awful feeling that no matter *what* I do, you couldn't care less. It's like scoring the game-winning touchdown, looking up, and seeing everyone in the stadium on their feet cheering, *except* the girl you're pinned to."

"Oh, Christ," moaned Sammy. "Come on, Thomas, drop the Yale Drama School crap. Of *course* I'm interested in everything you're doing. You know that as well as I do. I'm just trying to protect our home and our marriage. That's more important to me than all the deals you can make in a lifetime."

"Sammy," I said calmly, trying to avoid a scene before everyone from the office walked in, "let me try to explain it once more and—"

"You don't have to explain it once more, Thomas. I know the explanation well. You repeat it like a broken record." Sammy lit a cigarette and started again, mimicking my voice. " 'Samantha, you're just going to have to learn to put up with my strange working habits, and my associates, and the long hours, and the trips, and everything else. It's not going to last forever. I *swear* it won't. Soon I'll wrap it all up, and the three of us will go away and live happily ever after. It's just a few short years out of our life,' et cetera, et cetera.

"Tommy, that was fine when you were just starting out and you

152

weren't sure if your programs would be on the air from one week to the next. But it's different now. You're not a fly-by-night television producer anymore. You're the president of a large corporation that's going to be around for a long time, so stop telling me all of this craziness won't go on forever and that one of these days you're going to quit."

"Sammy, honey, that's the truth."

"It's *not* the truth, Tommy. It's a goddamn lie. You have no intentions of ever quitting. None whatsoever."

Sammy was getting upset. She only called me Tommy when she was either upset, or mad, or both.

"Tommy, you've been saying the same thing for two years now, and all your company does is grow bigger and bigger, and richer and richer, and all you become is more complicated, and more irritable, and more distant." Her eyes were beginning to well up.

"Sammy, listen. I love you. Just get off my back. I know the hours are crazy, and sometimes our privacy is shot to hell, and I don't see Caroline as much as you'd like me to, and things like that. I know it, but there's nothing I can do about it right now. I've got to keep striking while the iron's hot. The iron won't be hot forever. You've just got to mark time with me."

"That's all I've been doing, Tommy, is marking time. I mark time when you're not here and I mark time when you are. Do you know how horrible it is to live with someone whose mind is somewhere else? I'm tired of marking time, Tommy. I want to *enjoy* the time while we can. You earned it. Now let's enjoy the time together, like we used to do."

I chuckled a forced laugh. "Sammy, you talk like we're a hundred years old."

"For Christ sake, Tommy, we'll be a hundred by the time you decide to relax and have some fun with your life."

"I *am* having fun with my life."

"The *hell* you are!"

"Sammy, calm down."

"I don't *want* to calm down. I've been calm too long."

Sammy smashed her cigarette out and began walking around the room.

"Tommy, there's no end in sight. If you *really* want to know the truth, that's it. There is absolutely no end in sight. If your damn merger goes through, your company will be *twice* as big, with *twice* the problems, and you'll have a chain around your neck that will be *twice* as heavy." She lit another cigarette and waved the smoke away with her hand.

"How much money do you need, Tommy? How many magazine articles do you have to be in? How many employees do you have to carry, and how much do you have to pay for their loyalty and their smiles? How hardened do you have to become to avoid feeling bad knowing your so-called best friends are all talking about you behind your back? How many nights' sleep do you have to lose before you go into your office and fire somebody you've been carrying for years, only to find out later that he's been bad-mouthing you all over town?"

She stamped out her latest cigarette. If she lit another one, I was going to tell her she smoked too much.

"Tommy, in the beginning the company was Camelot. It was a commune. It was beautiful. All for one and one for all. Now it's a corporation that worries whether some clerk is sneaking long-distance phone calls. It's all changed, Tommy, and you're losing your beauty in the translation. You are. Goddamnit, sometimes I wish your damn television programs were flops. I wish they flopped and you had to take a lousy nine-to-five job, like you used to call it. Maybe then you wouldn't have changed so much. Once upon a time you were a sensitive, sweet man. But like your sister always says, shoulda, woulda, coulda."

She wiped her eyes and sat down.

In the silence that followed, I lowered my head. And then I thought, What am I ashamed of? What the bloody hell is she yelling at me for?

154

"What the bloody hell are you yelling at me for, Sammy? Are you yelling at me for working too hard? Are you yelling at me for being ambitious and trying to make something of myself? If that's what you're yelling at me for, then you ought to have your head examined."

I got up and walked over to where she was sitting. "I'm not a cheat or a scoundrel," I said, looking down at her. "I'm not some bum that sits around in his underwear shirt, drinking beer and smacking you in the face every other day. I'm working hard as hell, and succeeding, and you're crucifying me for it."

"I'm not crucifying you for anything," she said weakly.

"The hell you're not. All I ever hear from you, lately, is when am I going to quit? When are we going to go back to the good old days on Fortieth Street and Third Avenue."

"They *were* good old days."

"These are better days."

"They're not better days. In those days we had each other."

"We *still* have each other."

"We were dependent upon each other."

"We're *still* dependent upon each other."

"We're not. You're not dependent upon me anymore. Now you're dependent upon all of your lawyers and business managers and producers and secretaries and—"

"Cut it out, Sammy."

She stood up and put her arms around my waist, and her head on my shoulder.

"Thomas, when is it going to be just you and me, babe, again?"

"Aw, come on, Sammy. How many times do I have to tell you? I enjoy what I'm doing, I love everything about it, and I can't believe the success I'm having. But it can't last forever. And even if it does, that doesn't mean we can't be as happy as we were."

"When can we start, Thomas?"

"Start what?"

"Being as happy as we were?"

"Jesus, Sammy," I said, looking at her face, which suddenly had become fantastically pretty.

"When can we start?" she persisted.

"Now," I answered. "I'll make it like it used to be, Sammy. I really will." My words surprised me.

"Call Walt and Seymour and your secretary and tell them all to stay home," she said, kissing the tip of my nose.

"Okay."

"And then let's call your sister and curse, or just sit here in the living room and talk to each other. Or if you don't feel like talking, let's get in bed and snuggle and watch the roller derby."

Before I could decide what to do, the door chimes rang. It was Paul, and Walt, and Seymour, and David, and my secretary. They had come early.

I decided to get some work done.

"Do you have to pishy, Carrie?" I asked.

"Nope."

"Are you sure? You've had two orange drinks and a Coke."

"I'm sure."

Sure she's sure. Any minute there's going to be the inevitable yellow stream running down her leg and that crooked grin on her face.

"Can we see the hippos now, Daddy?"

"Posthaste."

"What?"

"Right away."

"Goody."

The hippos were napping. The water line of their pond covered everything but their eyes and noses.

"The hippos are napping, Carrie."

"Shit."

"What did you say?" I asked.

"I said shit."

"Well, put on some comfortable clothes and be downstairs in a half hour. My chauffeur will pick you up. I've had the cook make your favorite dish. We'll have a few drinks, we'll eat a delicious dinner, and we'll talk very little business."

"Fine."

"Half an hour," reminded Richard Clarke.

"I'll be ready. By the way, Richard, what *is* my favorite dish?"

"Veal piccata, right?"

"Right." I hated veal, but why hurt Richard's feelings.

Thirty minutes later, I was standing at the foot of the hotel's red carpet. Mr. Clarke's Rolls-Royce glided quietly to a halt in front of me and Mr. Clarke's chauffeur dashed around the rear of the car in a panic that I might open the door myself. I plopped into the back seat, right next to an exquisitely beautiful brunette woman.

"Hello," she said.

"Hello."

"You're Tommy."

"Yes, I am."

"I'm Joanna."

"Hello, Joanna."

Joanna was Richard Clarke's companion for the evening. His wife and kids lived in New York. Richard spent roughly half the year on the West Coast. I imagine spending half a year by yourself can become quite lonely.

I must say that Richard Clarke had exceptionally good taste. The only thing that confused me was what any girl could possibly see in Richard Clarke.

Richard Clarke's butler answered the door and showed us to the living room, where we were greeted by Richard Clarke and yet another exquisitely beautiful brunette woman. I was obviously wrong. Joanna was not Richard Clarke's companion for the evening. She was mine.

Rest and rehabilitation.

Alice in Wonderland.

Jesus H. Christ.

Someone handed me a drink. A butler delivered small hot dogs with toothpicks embedded in their skins. Richard Clarke took my arm and led me to a Picasso that he had just purchased.

"How do you like it?" he asked.

Alice in Wonderland.

"Richard, did you ever meet my wife, Sammy?"

Richard Clarke looked dumbfounded.

"Of course," he answered, his brows all furrowed up.

"Then you must know that I'm married."

Richard Clarke smiled the sickest smile I had ever seen in my life. "Tommy . . ." he began.

"If you *ever* do anything like this again, I'll pull my company out of your goddamn agency so fast, you won't know what hit you."

I handed Richard Clarke my drink and walked out of his house.

I climbed into bed. It had been a rough ten days since I returned from Los Angeles. I had worked every night until close to midnight.

"I'm tired, honey," I said. "I'm really exhausted."

I was getting undressed. Sammy was in bed drinking a cup of coffee and smoking a cigarette. She looked wide awake.

"How about a few hugs and kisses before we go to sleep?" she said.

"I'm too tired, honey, even for that."

I gave her a quick peck and slid under the covers.

"Good night, Sammy," I said, burrowing into my pillow.

"Good night," she answered.

I heard her put her coffee cup down.

I heard her put her cigarette out.

I heard her turn her light off.

"Honey," I said to my Sammy one morning at breakfast, "I really can't understand this constant frustration you keep putting yourself through. On one hand, you want to travel with me, you say you enjoy the trips, and you seem to look forward to them. But on the other hand, you hate being away from Caroline, and every time I suggest getting a woman for her, you get angry. If we had a woman that you could trust and were confident with, you wouldn't mind going with me. Carrie would be in good hands, we would be together, and everything would be fine."

Sammy looked up and stopped buttering her toast.

"I will *not* have a woman, as you call it. I had a woman when I was a child, only she was called a nanny then. Our daughter will not be brought up by a nanny. She'll be brought up by a mother, her mother. If it means that I can't go on business trips with you, then I just can't go."

"Then stop complaining when I leave," I said.

That morning I left for Europe.

The next day, in Paris, my secretary said, "I hope you didn't forget that it's your anniversary tomorrow."

"Oh, my God, I did! Jesus Christ, Sally, I thought I told you to remind me when my anniversary was coming up. Didn't I ask you to remind me?"

"Yes," answered my secretary politely. "I did. I reminded you ten days ago. I watched you write it down on a piece of paper and I saw you put the paper in your pocket.

"Anyway," she continued, "knowing how absent-minded you can be, I thought you might forget, so I had Jimmy go to Bonwit's and get your wife some Antilope spray *and* perfume. It *is* her favorite kind, you know."

I knew.

"I also told Jimmy to get a dozen roses, long-stemmed ones, and deliver the perfume and the roses to your apartment tomorrow at six o'clock. If you call your wife just before twelve o'clock our time, everything will arrive while you're talking to each other."

My secretary smiled. It was an expression that acknowledged efficiency. I smiled back.

"And when you have a minute," said my secretary politely, "maybe you can dictate a letter to your wife. If I send it out tonight, she'll receive it by tomorrow afternoon."

"Okay, Sally. But first make me a drink, will you, please?"

My secretary, Miss Sally Fitzpatrick, made my Scotch and soda better than anybody.

"Honey," I said, feeling a couldn't-care-less attitude about the company and all its niggling problems, "let's go do something together all day today. Just you and me, babe. Let's leave now and not come back until late tonight. Let's get away from the telephone, and let's stay away from places that people we know go to. Okay?"

"Okay," said Sammy, smiling.

"Where would you like to go?" I asked.

"To the zoo."

"To the *zoo!*"

"Yes, to the zoo."

It was an unusually cold gray September day in New York. I don't know what I had in mind when I suggested that Sammy and I go somewhere, but it certainly wasn't the zoo. So we went to the zoo.

Sammy held my hand, and we walked around the almost deserted mall. "Remember when we went to the zoo a long time ago, before we were married?" she asked.

"It wasn't that long ago."

"It seems like it was," she said wistfully. "Anyway, remember the mother gorilla and her new baby? I'll never forget how beautiful those two were together. I hope I'm as good a mother to my daughter as the gorilla was to her son. I wonder how they are. Let's go find them."

I bought a box of Cracker Jacks, and we looked for the mother gorilla and her son.

"There she is!" I said happily, pointing to a big gorilla.

"No it's not," said Sammy.

"How can you tell, Sam? All gorillas sort of look alike to me."

"I can tell, that's all. That one's not as cute. It doesn't have the bazazz the other one had."

We watched the gorilla for a few minutes, but its lack of bazazz disappointed Sammy, so we left.

"Look how beautiful he is," Sammy said at the polar bear's cage, "and frustrated, and awesome, and trapped. Just like you, honey."

"Very funny."

"Look how he paces back and forth, free, but not free at all, just like you-know-who. And look how we watch him, how our eyes follow him wherever he goes in wonder and terror, just like your employees' eyes follow you. And he knows we're talking about him behind his back, just like—"

"Come on, Sammy, cut it out."

I was beginning to feel sorry I didn't go to the office.

Sammy looked at my face and knew exactly what I was thinking. Her instincts were excellent.

"I'm sorry, Thomas. I won't tease you about the company anymore. I shouldn't have in the first place." She smiled and took my hand.

We had lunch in the zoo cafeteria. It, too, was almost empty, except for a few attendants and some elderly men, who always seem to sit in clusters at zoos and parks.

Sammy stirred her coffee and asked me, "If you had to come back to earth as an animal, which one would you choose?"

"I don't know."

"Think!"

I thought.

"A cow," I said.

"You're not serious," Sammy said. Her eyebrows came together in disbelief.

"I'm deadly serious."

"Why?"

"Why not? All you do all day is munch grass in a beautiful meadow until you're not hungry anymore, and then you go inside and somebody plays with your breasts."

"Hon-ey."

"How about you?" I asked.

"What animal would I like to be?"

"No. Can I play with your breasts?" I reached inside her coat and pinched one.

"Honey!"

She blushed. Sammy came from that old school of girls who still blushed.

"I'm blushing, aren't I?"

"Yes, you are."

She looked cute as hell.

"Sammy, you know what?"

"What?"

"You're so beautiful, it's sickening."

We had dinner at Saito. We ate Japanese style, sitting on the floor with our legs tangled in each other's under the table. At times I was terribly uncomfortable, and then there were moments when it was so cozy I almost fell asleep.

"Wake up, Thomas, and tell the lady what we want."

I ordered shrimp tempura, chicken and beef teriyaki, warm sake, and two bottles of cold Asahi beer.

Saito was one of our favorite restaurants. The chef behind the tempura bar was named Guysan. He liked us, and gave Sammy extra goodies with her shrimp. She would get a second eggplant, and occasionally two or three asparaguses. Sammy simply batted her eyelashes at Guysan and then smiled with delight when he dropped his little tidbits in her plate. I would smile, too, but he never gave me anything extra.

We ate our dinner with chopsticks. I hadn't used chopsticks often, and on my first try, I dropped a ton of beef teriyaki on my lap. Sammy tried to control herself, but she finally burst out laughing.

"Very funny," I said, looking at the mess between my legs.

I could always get a laugh out of Sammy and Caroline by suffering some small disaster. If I tripped on a curb, they would giggle. If I jammed the zipper on my fly, they wheezed. Once I bent over to clean up the mess our dog made in the kitchen, and the end of my tie fell into it. I left Sammy and our daughter gasping for air with that one.

"Well, how'd you like living a little today, you old fart?" asked Sammy. She was feeling giddy from the warm sake.

"I loved it," I said, and I did.

"Ready to say uncle?"

"What do you mean, uncle?"

"You know what I mean. I mean, are you ready to give up all that shit on Wall Street and come back to the good life at the zoo?"

"I love you, Sammy."

"I love you, too," she said softly.

"Happy anniversary, Mrs. Christian," I said on the telephone. "I was waiting for you to wake up, but this is as long as I can wait."

"I've been up for hours," Sammy said.

My secretary came in with some papers in her hand, but I waved her away. She signaled to me that they were important. I motioned to her to bring them to my desk, and I signed them as I talked.

"How's it feel to be married eight years, Sammy?"

"We're getting old, aren't we?"

"What do you want to do tonight?"

"Let's go to the zoo."

"Come on, Samantha, be serious. What do you want to do?"

"Let's stay home and I'll sketch you in the nude."

"Sammy, please be serious. If you had your choice of any place in the *entire* city of New York, where would you want to go most of all?"

"Guess what, Thomas? My mother died yesterday. The old witch kicked the bucket."

"Sammy, are you serious?"

"I'm very serious. She didn't wake up yesterday morning. My brother called and told me all about it. First time I've spoken to Ted in years. It's funny, but when he told me, I didn't feel a thing. Nothing. I couldn't have cared less. Strange not to care that your mother died. But I don't feel happy, either. I don't know what I feel."

There was a pause. She was probably lighting a cigarette.

"And guess what else? My brother says she left me a lot of money in her will. Like a couple of million dollars. I guess the rich just get richer, don't they?"

I heard her take a drag on her cigarette and blow out the smoke.

"Happy anniversary, Thomas."

"How's the new merger going?" asked Sammy.

"Okay, I guess."

I was getting undressed. Sammy was in bed drinking a cup of coffee and smoking a cigarette. She looked wide awake.

"Want to talk about it?" she asked.

"No, honey. I'm exhausted," I said, putting on my pajamas. "I'll tell you about everything tomorrow. Let's have dinner out somewhere and I'll bring you up to date."

"Thomas."

"What?"

I was getting angry. It had taken me years to break Sammy's habit of waking me in the middle of the night to talk about the day's problems. Now I was going to have to teach her that when

I came home from the office late, she should let me go right to sleep without any dutiful domestic conversation. It wasn't easy working fourteen-hour days and then having to come home and report in before being allowed to go to sleep.

"Thomas, I'm going to take Caroline and go to Mexico for a week or two. Are you listening?"

Yes, I was listening. I had slipped into bed with my back to Sammy, so she couldn't tell. "Yes, I'm listening."

"We'll stay at the Blums' house in Cuernavaca. Paul and Katie invited us down. I spoke to Katie last week. Actually, they invited the three of us down. You know that Paul's taking his vacation starting next week, so Katie thought you might want to get away, too, and that we could all stay at their house. Are you listening?"

"Yes, of course I'm listening."

"It's hard to tell, Thomas. Your back doesn't have any expressions. Is it possible that you could roll over and look at me?"

I rolled over.

"Do you want to go to Mexico for a week or so?" asked Sammy.

"I can't."

"I didn't think so," said Sammy, twirling her cigarette in her ashtray and watching the ashes fall off. "Anyway, Caroline and I will go. You'll be tied up with the merger, so it's probably a good time. What do you think?"

"I think it's a good idea," I said, noticing how happy I had begun to feel. My anger had disappeared, and I wasn't as sleepy as before. "It's a good time for you to go," I continued, sitting up and placing my pillows behind my back, "and I think it'll be good for Carrie, too."

Sammy was still looking at her ashes. "That's all I wanted to say. You can go to sleep now."

"It's all right," I said. "I'm not as tired as I thought. In fact, I'm hungry. Come with me to the kitchen and keep me company, and I'll make you one of Thomas C. Christian's famous omelets."

"Tommy?"

"What?"

Sammy was looking at me now. "You're actually happy that I'm going, aren't you? I mean bad happy, not good happy."

"What the hell does *that* mean?" I asked, knowing precisely what it meant.

"Nothing. Never mind. I'm not hungry, Tommy. I ate late tonight. You go and make your omelet. I'll read for a while."

I knew Sammy was hurt. I should have said something but I didn't.

I went to the kitchen and made an omelet. It tasted lousy. I didn't want it but I ate it anyway.

When I came back to the bedroom, Sammy was sleeping. Her face was always so cute when she slept. Her eyes were all crinkled up, her brow a little furrowed, her cheeks a little puffy. She looked adorable, peaceful, and loving.

By the end of the week, Sammy and Caroline had left for Mexico. They didn't stay for a week or two. Sammy rented a house and she and Caroline stayed for three months.

"I think your wife's cheating on you in Cuernavaca," Paul Blum told me one morning over coffee at the Sixth Avenue Delicatessen.

"Why do you say that?" I asked, trying to appear calm.

"I just think she is," he answered.

"But you're not *sure* she's cheating?" I asked. I suddenly felt very tired and it was only eight-thirty in the morning.

"If you mean did I catch her red-handed, no. But I have a pretty good feeling she is."

Alice in Wonderland.

Shoulda, woulda, coulda.

You and me, babe.

"It's a hell of a thing to hear first thing in the morning, huh?" Paul said, then he laughed. "I was thinking of waiting and telling you over ice cream tonight at Howard Johnson's, but I figured you wouldn't sleep, and you can use the sleep. Maybe by midnight you'll be so tired of thinking about this, you'll sleep." He laughed some more.

Paul had a spontaneous laugh that sounded hearty and good. It didn't always mean that something was funny. Sometimes he laughed to get rid of pressure or to lighten a serious point.

"I wrestled with this thing all night," he said. "I don't think I slept one single hour. I even called Katie."

Paul Blum's wife hated New York. She spent almost the entire year at their second home in Cuernavaca. Paul would visit her now and then, and occasionally he would stay for a week or two. Once Sammy and I went with him, and spent a long weekend as their house guests. That's when Sammy fell in love with Mexico.

"Look, Tommy, I could be all wrong. I could be, but I don't think I am. For the last month or so Sammy's been all aglow over one of those intellectual artist types. You know, the beard, the pipe, very artsy-craftsy. The antiestablishment anticapitalist with one of those nice family inheritances. You know the kind?"

I knew the kind.

"Every party she's invited to, he's there. Every party he's invited to, she's there. They don't come together, and they don't leave together. They just appear and disappear at the same time. You know what I mean?"

I knew what he meant.

"What really burns me up is when Katie and I go over to your house and *he*'s there. It's just the four of us, and I swear I only go not to hurt Sammy's feelings. The guy's a real pain in the ass, and besides, the whole thing burns me up, but I don't want to aggravate Sammy."

It would burn me up, too.

"Maybe she's getting even with you, Tommy."

"For what?"

"I don't know," said Paul Blum. "Maybe she's *not* getting even with you. Maybe she's getting even with her family. Maybe she married you to get even with her family in the first place, because she knew it would burn them up, and now that you're a success, she's trying to find another bum and burn them up again."

Maybe she was. I never thought of that.

"Anyway, I had to tell you, Tommy. It's been bothering me and I had to get it off my chest. I need my sleep, too," Paul said, and he laughed again. "But like I said, I'm not a hundred percent sure; I could be wrong."

"I could be wrong," I said to Sammy, "but I think I know what you want to talk about."

"I really don't think you do," she answered.

Sammy had returned from Mexico the day before.

We were having dinner at Mimi's restaurant. We decided to go there for old times' sake, and because Sammy wanted to tell me something. She said she wanted to save it until we were at Mimi's.

Mimi was glad to see us. We tried to remember when we were there last, and just the fact that we had to think about it was distressing to all of us. Mimi showed us a picture of his new baby. It was a handsome child with blond hair and blue eyes, destined to drown in a swimming pool two years later. Mimi would get a heart attack trying to rescue the baby. He would recover, and life would go on, ooblah dee, ooblah dah.

"It's funny that Mimi would show us a picture of his new kid tonight," said Sammy, lighting a cigarette.

"Why? What's so funny about that?"

"It just is. Why don't you order yourself a drink?"

"Because I don't want a drink. What is it you want to talk about?"

"I think you should have a drink before we start talking," she said, and called Mimi.

Mimi took our drink order and left. The conversation had come to a halt and would obviously stay that way until he came back. Sammy was smiling her forced smile, and so was I. We were

170

marking time and it was uncomfortable. This is foolish, I told myself.

"Sammy, this silence is foolish. I know what you're going to talk about, or at least I have a pretty good idea, so let's talk about it and get it over with."

Sammy's elbows were on the table and her chin rested on her knuckles.

"What am I going to talk about?" she asked.

"You're going to tell me you were having an affair in Cuernavaca." There, I said it.

"Thomas, drink your drink," Sammy said quietly.

"Then you *weren't* having an affair in Cuernavaca?"

"Thomas, I'm pregnant."

"Pregnant!"

"Yes."

"You are?"

"Yes, I am."

Pregnant! A *fait accompli.* Then if it was a *fait accompli,* what the hell were we going to discuss? And why the hell didn't we discuss it in the first place, unless it was an accident?

"Was it an accident?"

"Of course it was, but accidents do happen, you know."

Okay, it was an accident. Jesus, Mother, Mary and Joseph, accidents do happen, you know. Goddamnit, why am I so depressed? So we're having a baby. Great! We'll have a baby.

"Okay, so it was an accident. So what? It's great! It's about time we had another kid."

"It's *not* great, Thomas. I don't *want* to have it!"

"You don't want to have it?"

"That's right, I don't want to have it." Sammy leaned across the table toward me and whispered, "Please keep your voice down, Tommy." And then, more to herself, "I *knew* we should have talked about this at home."

"It was *your* idea to come here," I said angrily.

"I know. Can I have another glass of wine, please?"

I ordered another glass of wine, and then Sammy said, "Tommy, I want an abortion." She whispered the word "abortion." After she said it, her eyes darted to the other booths to see if anybody was listening.

"Tommy, say something."

"I don't know what to say." I didn't. An abortion. Why the hell would she want an abortion?

I saw my old friend Gil Mack as soon as I walked in the door. He was sitting across the room at a crap table, and I was deliriously happy to see him.

"Hi ya, sport," he whooped, dropping his chips and wrapping his arms around me like a bear.

"Hello, Gil."

"What the hell are you doing in London, Tommy? Buying the Bank of England?"

"Cut it out," I said, and we walked to the bar.

I had come to England to look at a play that was opening in Oxford. I had heard some good things about it, and was thinking of taking an option on the stage and film rights.

It was cold and dreary in London, and the drive to Oxford had been endless. I drove with boring people, the play was boring, and the party after the play was boring.

The drive back to London had taken an eternity.

After saying good night to my host and hostess, a moment I thought would never arrive, I had dashed off to a private club for a drink that I desperately needed. The club was the Black Cat. It was on Curzon Street, not far from the freezing flat Sammy and I had found when we first came to Europe. I saw Gil when I walked in the door.

Gil and I sat at the bar and talked for hours. We discussed family and business, and friends and enemies. We examined old memories, invented new ones, told boring stories, and entertained each other as only good friends can.

Gil had changed. His evolution during the past nine years had surprised everyone who knew him, his family most of all.

Gil's parents had simply been waiting until their playboy son was sentenced to prison for a particularly revolting and heinous crime they wouldn't understand, just after he married a thirteen-year-old prostitute addicted to a drug they never heard of.

But Gil fooled them.

He married Sally Starbuck, heir to one of the largest brewery fortunes in the Midwest. And then Gil's father died, and Gil had to take over the family business.

As corporate head of the Mack Candy Company, Gil showed a side of himself nobody had ever suspected was there, not even Gil. He ran the company with style and grace, a thrilling sort of drive, and a hard cunning inherent in reprobates, outcasts, whores, beach bums, and pimps when the opportunity to go straight and make something of themselves appears and the desire to do so rumbles through their bones.

In the years since Mimi's and Martha's Vineyard, Gil Mack had come full cycle from a good-for-nothing wastrel to a successful businessman, a devoted son, and a loving husband.

"So we both were supposed to be ne'er-do-wells, and we fooled them," said Gil. "I wonder what that proves?"

"Beats the shit out of me," I answered.

"I'll tell you what it proves," Gil said, slurring his words somewhat. "It proves that there are no rules and no answers. It proves that to move into another state of being necessitates a change of beliefs, that the eternal struggle in art is to forget everything but the essential, and that assumptions harden into fact, so assume the best."

"It also proves that you must be careful what you pray for because you may get it," I said, waving for another drink. "And it proves that when the going gets tough, the tough get going."

"Bravo!" said Gil, jumping off his bar stool. He tucked his thumb into his vest and attempted a professorial stance. "It also proves that the present does *not* recede into the past. It advances into the future to confront you."

"Magnificent," I said, still waving for my drink.

"And," bellowed Gil, causing a bit of a scene, "it *also* proves that there's no use hurrying unless you're sure the train you're catching is the right one."

"And that fifty percent of something is better than a hundred percent of nothing."

"And that if you can't get dinner, get a sandwich."

"And that we live because we live," I said, playing with my drink.

"Yes," said Gil, sitting down again. "We live because we live."

We walked out of the Black Cat at ten o'clock in the morning, and had to stand in the doorway for a few minutes to let our eyes adjust to the sunlight.

"Come with me," I said to Gil. "I want to buy you a present."

"Goody."

"But you have to buy me one, too, and money's no object."

"Okay," said Gil, his eyes a deep red, his ascot askew.

We walked down to Bond Street. Gil bought me an eight-dollar hat at Hillhouse & Company, and I bought him a pretzel.

"Not very imaginative," said Gil.

"Who asked you?"

We took a taxi to the Hotel Connaught and sat at the bar comparing gifts.

"I've been had," concluded Gil, brushing the last of the pretzel crumbs off his lap. "And besides, it's downright dastardly to sit in the Hotel Connaught with debris in your crotch. It's un-English."

The Hotel Connaught bar was about as English as you could get. It was austere in the pure sense of the word. The room was a stern place, severely simple, stringently moral; characteristics not particularly admirable for a bar. Yet the place reeked of so much tradition and charm that it was pleasant drinking there, and that's where Gil and I ended up discussing the decision I had to make.

"So what do you think, Gil?"

"Like I said before, Tommy, I think you're crazy to ask me what I think, but since you really want to know, I think you're nuts!"

I had told Gil that I had an opportunity to sell my company. If the deal went through, as planned, I would be able to put millions of dollars in the bank, retire from the world of business, and fulfill my promise to my wife. Sammy, Carrie, and I would then theoretically live happily ever after.

"I really think you're nuts," continued Gil. "You're only what? Thirty-two?"

"Thirty-four."

"Okay, thirty-four. You're only thirty-four years old. You're not ready to retire, and besides, you enjoy working. You enjoy doing just what you're doing: wheeling and dealing, keeping ten pots boiling on the stove, surprising yourself by accomplishing things you never imagined you could do. It would be a shame to give all that up now. Sammy should understand that."

Gil took my new green tweed hat and put it on his head. The bartender came by and asked him to take it off. Gil took it off, but when the bartender walked away, he put it on again.

The bartender returned. I knew he would, and I looked the other way when he approached us. Once again he asked Gil to remove my hat from his head, and suggested checking it in the lobby. Gil asked the bartender if he liked the hat. The bartender said it was nice. He also said that if Gil put it on again, he was going to ask him to leave. He said it firmly but pleasantly.

"I wonder what Mike Malloy would have said?" I asked Gil after the bartender left.

"About what?"

"About selling my company."

"He would have said you'd be goddamned insane to do it."

"I'm afraid if I don't sell the company, Sammy's going to leave me."

"Then let her go, goddamnit."

Gil politely indicated to the bartender that we wanted another round of drinks.

When they came, I looked at mine intently, as though there were answers somewhere at the bottom. I jiggled the glass and watched the ice cubes rock back and forth in the Scotch.

"She's making you choose. That's what she's doing, you know?"

"Choose?" I asked.

"Yes. Sammy's making you choose between her and your company. She's forcing you to make a choice. Your company's a big part of your life, Tommy, and if you don't admit it, you're a hypocrite. And if Sammy can't understand that, then she's just plain stupid."

Gil continued to poke at the lemon in his gin and tonic. It was my turn to talk.

"If Sammy were here, she'd make a good case about how rotten a husband and father I've become. I'm sure your average jury would hang me in a minute. Every now and then I look at myself in a mirror and say, Hey, maybe you *are* an old bastard. Maybe you *should* be paying more attention to your family. Maybe you should be coming home early, and putting on slippers, and patting your daughter on the head, and kissing your wife's cheek, and asking, What's for dinner? Maybe I should be fixing things around the house, and going down to the hardware store to get some hooks for the closet."

I took a long swallow of Scotch.

"But every time I think about that I think, Bullshit, I don't want to go to any goddamn hardware store and get any goddamn hooks."

And then I started to laugh, and so did Gil.

"Bloody hooks," said Gil, wheezing and cackling all over the place.

176

"Bloody hooks," I said, falling onto the bar, howling help-lessly. Oh, God, I laughed. I laughed so hard, I was in terrible pain. When I looked up, Gil had my silly hat on his head again. I fell back onto the bar, a spastic wreck.

The bartender came over, just as we knew he would, and asked us to leave, just as we knew he would.

"I love you, Gil."

"I love you, too, old sport."

Gil gulped down the rest of his drink, tipped my hat to the bartender, and put his arm around my shoulders. I put my arm around Gil's shoulders, and we left.

We walked through Hyde Park singing "Bloody hooks" to the tune of "Silent Night."

I decided to finance a movie about Montez.

Montez was the best and richest matador in the world. He owned eight Mercedes Benz automobiles, a Jaguar, a Rolls-Royce, and a magnificent yacht that was permanently anchored in Nice. He also had eleven million dollars in cash and the second biggest finca in Spain.

And he was illiterate.

He couldn't write his name, but he piloted his own plane, a twin-engine Cessna with the name MONTEZ in bright orange on its side.

Montez was small and thin and charming. He had a boyish face, with rumpled brown hair and an amazing grin. He looked com-monplace in pajamas and he wore street clothes badly, but he was devastating in his suit of lights.

In the bullring, he became papal; a hero wonder that cut across all ages and sexes. He was the Maestro, the man every boy wanted to grow up to be and every woman wanted to love. "Oh, dear God, I wish he would look at *me* like he looks at that bull," moaned a pretty woman sitting next to me in Seville.

Montez was a generous, simple, unpretentious man. He was

also bloodthirsty and violent. Killing was his profession, and he loved his work.

For nine months of the year he slaughtered three bulls a day. His fee was five thousand dollars a bull.

The other three months of the year he relaxed by killing deer, elk, wild pigs, and wolves in the mountains of Spain.

When he shot skeet on his ranch in Seville, he used live pigeons instead of plastic or clay disks. He would bark a signal, a servant would step on the trap release, and the pigeon would be propelled into the air. Montez would let it start to fly and then blast it to bits with his double-barreled shotgun. The Maestro would laugh every time he destroyed a pigeon. He would be sullen if he missed.

Sammy and I went to Guadalajara, Pamplona, Madrid, Cordoba, and Seville to see Montez perform. Neither of us had seen a bullfight before.

Montez was unbelievable. He brought the bulls to us and killed them in front of our seats. He threw Sammy the ears and tails. Their blood stained her dresses. At one fight, Sammy ran out of the stadium and threw up. At another she almost fainted. She began to hate every minute of the Montez project.

In Seville, she left.

She flew to Barcelona with a girl she didn't like named Cheryl. Cheryl was a playgirl from New York whose latest fads were matadors and leather coats. Cheryl told Sammy that Barcelona had marvelous leather things, so that's where they went.

Sammy bought a leather coat in Barcelona, and flew back to the United States. She was glad to get home to her daughter. She was delighted to forget the bulls and the swords and the blood bubbling out of the animals' mouths; horses blinded and terrorized, urinating from the pain of horns jammed into their ribs; dead beasts being dragged away by chains; ears falling into her lap.

I remember the night Sammy flew to Barcelona.

It was after the fight in Seville. We were waiting for Montez to dress. Sammy told me she was going home. I was relieved. I knew how much she had come to hate Montez, the constant killing, the violent atmosphere.

Montez drove us to the airport. I kissed Sammy good-bye. She went with that stupid girl to a small plane I had chartered. I watched the plane taxi out to the runway. I didn't see her take off. The Maestro was in a hurry.

On the road back to Madrid, Sammy's plane flew over our car. It was a strange and eerie sensation to be driving down an empty Spanish highway in the dead of night and suddenly see the plane you hired, with your wife in it, pass overhead. Before it passed, just for an instant, my car and Sammy's plane hung together, one on top of the other. They seemed to touch, and pause, and then detach and continue on their lonely, separate ways. And then Sammy's little plane disappeared in the black night, and soon all you could hear was the solid, confident drone of Montez's gray Mercedes.

I knew then that I would lose my Sammy.

I knew it that night, driving from Seville to Madrid, with the world's bravest and richest matador.

Sammy called and wanted to have lunch.

The restaurant we went to was filled with well-dressed, well-fed people. The headwaiter showed us to our table. It wasn't very private. We sat side by side, along a row of other people sitting side by side. I ordered a tall Scotch and soda, with a twist. Sammy wanted tomato juice.

"Tommy," she said.

"What?"

"I want a divorce."

She said it just like that.

Sammy and I walked through Central Park. We took one path, then another. We had nowhere to go. We had no direction to take. We had no future. We had no past. We had nothing.

We sat down on a bench.

It reminded me of the green bench we had sat on in the small park near Sammy's house in Greenwich. When we sat on that bench, many years ago, autumn leaves swirled around our feet. Earlier that day, Mr. Wilkerson had called me an opportunist, and Mrs. Wilkerson said I was marrying Samantha for her money. Sammy sat shivering at my side on that cold Sunday afternoon. We were both desolate then.

We were both desolate again.

Why was I so sad? Didn't I want a divorce, too?

"Sammy," I said, finding it difficult to talk, "let's not get a divorce. Let's just separate. You go your way and I'll go mine. You live your life, and I'll live mine. Date other men, *live* with other men, but let's not get a divorce. It's such a hassle to get a divorce. Lawyers and papers, and all of the heartache that goes with it."

"No."

"Sammy, listen. It has to be pure torture for two people like us to go through a divorce. Sammy, we've never even *discussed* it before. We've just let our marriage drift to where you look up one afternoon at lunch and say, 'I want a divorce.' Maybe we'll miss each other. Maybe a separation will do us good. We may realize we need each other."

"No."

"Sammy, please, let's just separate. Let's do it for six months, a year, two years, whatever." I heard my voice begging, pleading with her. "Sammy, if we get a divorce, I'm afraid we'll never go back to each other again. I'm afraid, Sammy, and just don't sit there and say no, like a broken record."

"No! No! *No!*" she said.

The man sitting at the next bench looked at us over his newspaper.

"No," repeated Sammy. "You're either married or you're not. There is no in-between. We each have a life to live. We cannot go on together in any way, shape, or form, and that's *that!*"

180

Sammy lit a cigarette. I noticed her hand was shaking.

"I'm a nervous wreck," continued Sammy, "you're a nervous wreck, and Carrie's a nervous wreck. We'll all end up hating each other. No, we will *not* separate. If it doesn't work, if we find we need each other like you said, we can always remarry, but we will *not* just separate."

We walked back to our apartment. I took off my coat, pulled down my tie, and fell into an armchair. Sammy lit a cigarette, and paced back and forth.

"I can't believe this *entire* thing," she said. "I really can't believe it. You and me. Who would have thought that we would get a divorce? Who would have *ever* thought that? Would you? I wouldn't. But we are!"

I didn't know what to say.

"I can't believe it," whispered Sammy. She was talking to herself. "I just can't believe it."

And then she turned and looked at me, and I knew that at that moment in her life, she hated me.

"*You* of all people," she said, her eyes squinting. "You turned out to be just like my father. Mergers, acquisitions, board meetings, stockholders meetings, sales meetings, public relations meetings, legal meetings. Meetings, meetings, meetings. Never any time for anything but business. Everything in your life now is business. Accounts payable, accounts receivable, profits, losses, earnings, shares."

Sammy fell into a couch and continued talking to some imaginary spot on the living room wall. I suddenly became a third person, an eavesdropper to her conversation.

"He always had time for his meetings, but never enough time for his daughter's birthday parties, or our anniversary. He had time to personally pick out a company Christmas gift, but he had to send his secretary to find something for his wife. He always had time to have dinner with any number of clients and customers, half of whom he never knew, but he never had time to take me to dinner, alone, just the two of us. Oh, that's not entirely fair. We did have dinners out, alone, sometimes whole days together, but when it happened he made me feel like I was the luckiest woman on earth. Christ, it got so that when we made love, it was a national event!"

"Sammy."

"Don't Sammy me!" she shouted, and then she quickly composed herself. "Look, Tommy, just don't Sammy me. You don't know how you've changed. You refuse to believe it when I say so. You won't believe it no matter *who* says so, but you have. You *have!* I've told you a million times. I tried to get it into your head for the last year, but all you did was get annoyed. You used to be sweet, Tommy. Sweet, and sensitive, and gentle. You used to love life, and you used to love to live. You had your values all in the right places. You had ideals, scruples, honor, and respect for yourself and for others. But no more.

"Now you're a tense, taut machine that has to perform. Every day you get up, you have to perform. First it was your family, then me, then your employees, then your board of directors, then your stockholders. Now it's your public. Well, fine, Tommy, fine. Keep right on performing, only do it without me. I'm tired of seeing you perform. I can't stand watching it anymore. I can't stand seeing you rip yourself apart for some unknown audience that won't give two shits when they put you away. I just can't stand it anymore. *I just can't stand it!"*

Sammy sat down on an ottoman, put her head in her hands, and talked to the floor.

"Guess what, Tommy?"

"What?"

"I saw a big black Carey Cadillac go by the day before yesterday. A very important executive was sitting in the back, reading a *Wall Street Journal.* He never looked out of the window once. He had absolutely no desire to look at people, or store windows, or anything. Just his lousy *Wall Street Journal.* And guess what?"

"What?"

"The man in the big black Carey Cadillac was you, Tommy! The man was *you!*"

Sammy ran to the bathroom and slammed the door shut. I heard her crying. She cried and cried and cried. I got up and walked back and forth. She was still crying.

I went to the bathroom and stood by the door.

"Stop crying, Sammy," I pleaded. "Please. I can't stand to hear you cry." But she didn't stop.

I couldn't bear it anymore. I opened the door.

Sammy was sitting on the toilet. Her panties were down around her ankles, her shoulder was leaning against the wall, her face was staring at the ceiling. She was sobbing.

She was sobbing her heart out on the cold toilet, with her panties down around her ankles.

That's what I had brought my Sammy to.

A little over a year later I walked into Saint Patrick's Cathedral and sat for a while. Nothing happened, so I left.

I wandered down Fifth Avenue, crossed in front of the Plaza Hotel, and entered Central Park at Fifty-ninth Street. It was a glorious January afternoon, sunny and not too cold. It was a good day for walking.

I stopped at the ice skating rink, but it was between sessions, so I stood and watched the remnants of the ten-to-one crowd leave. Two attendants were getting ready to skate around the ice, clearing away sliced-up snow and debris with their shovels. Their endless circling bored me, so I went to the zoo.

The zoo.

"Look how beautiful he is," Sammy had said at the polar bear's cage, "and frustrated, and awesome, and trapped. Just like you, honey."

The polar bear was still there, still pacing in one direction, turning abruptly, and pacing back again.

It was in front of that agitated polar bear that I decided to sell my company. The offer I had received was too big to turn down. Anyway, I was tired.

"You want to be the richest guy in the cemetery?" Geraldine had warned.

Nope. Besides, I wanted another crack at that elusive Great American Novel.

In any case, that day in front of the polar bear—the day I decided to sell my company—would have been Sammy's and my tenth wedding anniversary. Ain't life funny? Now I would finally have time to smell flowers with Sammy and slide on my stomach in Central Park with Carrie, but Sammy and Carrie wouldn't be around.

Maybe I should have sold the company sooner?

Maybe Sammy should have stuck it out a little longer?

Shoulda, woulda, coulda, like my sister used to say.

A short, curt note came in the mail. It said, "I would appreciate the opportunity to meet with you."

It was signed John T. Wilkerson.

I met Samantha's father for lunch at "21".

"I understand now," said Mr. John T. Wilkerson, pushing a butter dish around with his hand, "that when I turned my back on Samantha, she had no one until you came along. Now that you've left her, she has no one at all."

"I wouldn't say that Sammy has no one at all, sir. And by the way, she left me."

"Whatever," said Mr. Wilkerson, dismissing my last comment lightly. "It just worries me."

"It's not that serious, sir. Sammy certainly doesn't have any financial worries, and she still has me in emergencies. Besides, I'm sure she'll find someone else soon," I said, feeling a sharp pain in my stomach when I said it. "As you know, sir, your daughter is a very attractive and very eligible woman."

184

Mr. John T. Wilkerson continued playing with his butter dish, and without looking up, he said, "Is there a chance the two of you might go back together again?" He said it as though he wished there was.

"I doubt it."

"Why? Don't you two love each other anymore?"

"Yes, I think we love each other, very much. We just can't live together."

"That's a shame. I'm truly sorry to hear you say that," said Mr. John T. Wilkerson, retired president and chairman of the board of the American Steel Corporation, and presently an active board member of numerous funds, charities, hospitals, foundations, and institutions.

It was the same Mr. John T. Wilkerson who, many years ago, had pointed his finger at me and called me an opportunist. He also banned me from his house and asked me never to see his daughter again. In fact, he didn't ask me, he forbade me.

He also disinherited his daughter when she disobeyed him and married me.

He was the same Mr. John T. Wilkerson who had prevented Sammy from buying more than three maternity dresses. Well, he didn't actually prevent her, I guess, but who cares now? A lot of water had run under the bridge, or dam, or whatever water runs under. And besides, many things had happened to all of us, including Mr. John T. Wilkerson. His wife had died, he had suffered two heart attacks, and he had become a seemingly lonely, guilty, sad man. I realized, seeing Mr. John T. Wilkerson for the first time since the day I married his daughter, that I felt sorry for him.

"I guess you know that Sammy never liked her mother," said Mr. Wilkerson.

"That's probably because your wife never liked Sammy," I said, and was immediately sorry I said it. "I'm sorry, Mr. Wilkerson. I shouldn't have said that."

"That's all right, Mr. Christian," said Sammy's father, still playing with his butter dish. "Mrs. Wilkerson was, well, she was . . ." he paused, and then he said, "hard at times."

I was surprised to hear Mr. Wilkerson say that, and then again, maybe I wasn't.

We ate for a few minutes, and then Mr. Wilkerson said, "I understand that Samantha was seeing a man behind your back in Mexico."

"I can't say for sure," I answered.

"If she *had* been seeing a man behind your back, could you forgive her?"

I looked at him.

He looked at me, and smiled.

I was about to answer, when the chairman of the board of the Pacific Refining Company stopped to say hello. When he left, Mr. Wilkerson thoughtfully changed the subject.

"If I may be extremely presumptuous, I would like to ask a favor of you."

"Certainly. What?" I asked.

"Bring Sammy and me back together again."

Mr. Wilkerson surprised me for the second time.

"As I said before," continued Mr. Wilkerson, "Samantha doesn't forgive easily. She refuses to return my phone calls, and hasn't answered any of my letters. I've been calling and writing her for almost a year now. I am fully aware that she has a good reason to be bitter, but I would like to see her and talk to her again. I would also like to meet my granddaughter. You might say that I have a desire to tie up several loose ends, before it's too late."

The waiter brought our coffee.

"I'm sure Samantha would listen to you," said Mr. Wilkerson. "I'm sure she would accept your phone call. I would appreciate it if you would let her know that I would like to see her, and how important it is to me that I do."

Walking out of "21," Mr. Wilkerson said, "I understand that

186

after Samantha married you, her asthma never troubled her again. Is that true?"

I told Mr. Wilkerson that it was true.

"She really hated us, didn't she?" he said. He looked tired.

Before Mr. Wilkerson stepped into his limousine, he said, "Thank you. I know your time is valuable, and I feel quite certain that you must have had some second thoughts about seeing me. I can only say that I appreciate your coming, and I hope you understand the importance of my seeing Samantha again."

And then he said, "I apologize, Mr. Christian, for my actions toward you in the past, and I sincerely hope you see it clear to forgive me." And then, almost as an afterthought, he said, "And I sincerely hope that someday you see it clear to forgive Samantha, too, if—and I repeat, *if*—there is anything to forgive."

And then Mr. John T. Wilkerson drove off.

I called Sammy, and she promised to speak to her father.

Part 4

"*Y*ou have a beautiful house," said the blond actress as we drove up to my front door. She was right. It *was* a beautiful house, and it was the only right thing the idiot had said all night.

It had been exactly a year and a half since Sammy and I separated. In the divorce settlement, I gave Sammy our apartment in New York and our homes in Paris and Bermuda. She rented the Paris home to a Belgian family and sold the house in Bermuda.

After I sold the company, I moved to Los Angeles and stayed in our small apartment there, until I found a house. When I did, I let the apartment go.

I searched for my house for over a month. I had definite requirements. The house had to be on a cliff overlooking the ocean. It had to be in an area where the neighbors' houses were a good distance away, and where you were able to ride horses. It had to be a relatively small house with a large living room and fireplace, a comfortable kitchen, a large master bedroom and fireplace, and a small second bedroom for my daughter, when she came to visit. I found that exact house just above Malibu, almost in Trancas.

It was a solid, rustic ranch house, built by the man who sold it to me. The house was on three acres of land, completely surrounded by thick impenetrable trees, except on the ocean side. There, a cliff dropped jaggedly to the beach below.

191

Every kind of fruit tree blossomed around the property: orange, olive, peach, pear, avocado. On the land was a corral and a run-down guesthouse that I didn't bother to repair.

After I moved in, I built a wooden fence seven feet high and battened at the seams. The fence circled the entire property.

"Having trouble with prowlers?" asked a concerned neighbor.

"No. With friends," I answered.

The only things I truly loved, since leaving Sammy, were my daughter and my house.

"Why do you live all the way out here?" asked the blond actress. She was making an effort to be interested in me.

"To be alone, to find peace, and to try to write again," I answered. As if she cared. It was always such a chore talking to these buttercups. That's what Mike Malloy used to call stupid idiotic nymphets, like the little brainless blonde standing next to me.

Buttercups.

The all-American beauty roses who fluttered false eyelashes over vacant eyes, who smiled cheerless smiles that revealed Pepsodent square teeth, who carried their toothbrushes in their purses, and had the mentality of a box of Tampax.

Buttercups.

"To be *alone!* Oh, *that's* a good one," said the blond actress, giggling and fluttering, and smiling cheerlessly. "From what I hear, being alone is *not* one of your problems. I hear your bed is like a Hilton hotel." She looked at me coyly.

Buttercups, Mike used to call them. Little fucking buttercups.

I did intend to live alone, but I couldn't. I wanted to be a recluse, riding at dawn, writing most of the day, walking the beaches at sunset. Perhaps a dinner date with a charming, witty, interesting woman. Perhaps an occasional ribald evening with a ribald girl. Occasional.

But it hadn't worked out that way. I had been spending most of my time with buttercups.

It was the loneliness.

I wasn't able to cope with the loneliness. Loneliness would allow me to think, and I didn't want to think.

"Where should I put my coat?" asked the blond actress.

"On the floor."

You play tennis against a lousy tennis player, you play like a lousy tennis player. You talk to an idiot, you talk like an idiot.

"Oh, my God, what a cozy, warm place," said the blond actress. "I mean, it's *super* cozy here. I could stay for days and days."

I do stay here for days and days, I said to myself. The days are all right. It's the nights. The nights are murder. Why is that? I wondered. Why do I begin suffering about five o'clock? Why do my spirits and the sun drop simultaneously? Actually, it should be the best part of the day. It's the time when I can build a fire in the living room, make my Scotch and soda with a twist, just the way I like it, and relax and read all the good books and magazines I've saved. But it never works that way, I thought. It just never works that way.

"Who's this?" asked the blond actress, pointing to a picture of my daughter on the mantel over the fireplace in the living room.

"That's my daughter."

"Cute," said the blond actress.

That's what they all said. Cute. She's a cute one. Golly, she's cute. My, she's cute. Sometimes they would say she looks like me.

"She looks like *you!*" discovered the blond actress, batting her eyes and showing her big, fine, square, cavity-free white sparkling teeth.

I missed my daughter painfully. She was the cause of most of my terrifying moments when the sun went down and I was alone and could think, even though I didn't want to.

"Who's *this!*"

"That's my wife."

"I thought you said you were divorced," said the blond actress, slowly and deliberately, showing some theatrical concern, as if it mattered.

"I am," I said, as if it mattered.

"Then why do you still call her your wife?"

"What would you rather I call her?"

"Your ex-wife, or your former wife," the buttercup answered. "My God, but you have a lot of pictures of her. Are these pictures of her, too?"

"Yes."

"My God."

My God, I *did* have a lot of pictures of a woman who legally wasn't a part of my life anymore, didn't I? They were everywhere. In the living room. In the kitchen. Even in the bedroom.

"My God, they're even in the bedroom," said the blond actress. "I think you have an ex-wife fetish or something. Will you make a fire here, Tommy? I think it would be super to have a fire here."

The picture of Sammy in the bedroom happened to be a particularly good one, I thought. It was a picture that constantly bothered the buttercups. All of Sammy's pictures bothered the buttercups, but the one in the bedroom bothered them the most.

One time, after an unusually nasty telephone conversation with Sammy, I went about the house taking all her pictures off the walls and tables. I put them in a large cardboard box and I put the box in the garage. Every time I looked at the box, it annoyed me. Pictures of Sammy and me in New York, our wedding picture, pictures of us in Saint Tropez, and with the baby just after she was born; pictures like that weren't meant to be in a dirty cardboard box stuck in some greasy corner of the garage.

I took the box back into the house and hung all the pictures up again. When I did, I noticed how beautiful Sammy had become as she grew older.

"Well," said the blond actress, "what'll we do now?"

What'll we do now? The ritual was about to begin. How would I handle this one? How did she want it handled? It shouldn't be a problem, I said to myself. I had an assortment of approaches, collected from nearly two years of experience.

Tommy the lover.

"Aw, come on," Mike Malloy once said to me at Mimi's restaurant, when I was still a bachelor. "You're only a lover depending on who you love. You can make it with buttercups six days a week, and twice on Sunday, and you won't impress me. I don't think romancing a beast or a buttercup who can't spell her name is any kind of accomplishment. The guy that can make it with one woman who has intelligence and beauty and class is a greater lover to me than the guy who makes it with twenty buttercups. It all depends on the way you look at it."

It all depends on the way you look at it.

"This is *nice*," said the blond actress. We were lying in bed naked. The fire was crackling, and there was a glass of red wine on each night table.

This is nice. That's what they all said. This is nice.

How many had there been, lying on their back naked on the left side of the bed, their right hand under their head, their left hand holding the wineglass, their eyes turned slightly to the left, looking at the fire?

Countless?

Yes, countless. Every day? Well, not every day, but certainly every week, except the weeks my daughter came to visit.

My daughter.

Someday she would be my best friend.

Someday she would forget all the moments I didn't have time for her because I didn't want to be bothered.

I didn't want to be bothered.

What could I have been doing that was so important that I didn't want to be bothered? Why was I too bothered to take a walk with her, or to read her a story, or to kiss a bruise?

Too bothered.

Could you be a best friend to somebody who was too bothered to be your best friend?

I doubt it, I said to myself. I doubt it.

"Don't leave, *please!*" she sobbed when she was six. "Please, Daddy, don't go away. Please! *Please!*"

She ran to the door of the apartment and bolted the chain, but I left anyway, behind my chauffeur and the elevator man, who were carrying my bags and suitcases to the car.

But wasn't that the way Sammy wanted it?

"Please, Daddy, please. *Please!*"

I heard my daughter crying until the elevator doors closed.

I felt my stomach turn. Jesus Christ almighty, was I going to have to relive those scenes for the rest of my life?

"Why do I have to go home now?" my daughter asked when she was seven. The Christmas vacation was over, and I was putting her on a plane back to New York. "Please, Daddy, don't send me home. Why can't I stay with you? Why can't I go to school here? Why can't I live in your house with you? Please don't send me home."

I handed my daughter to a stewardess. The stewardess was embarrassed. So was I.

"Please don't send me home, Daddy. Please! *Please!*" And then in anger, "Why did Mama and you get a divorce in the first place?" And then somewhere down the companionway I heard her cry out, "Please, Daddy, stay with me. Please! *Please!*"

I heard her crying even after she disappeared. I heard her crying until she was far enough away that I couldn't hear her crying anymore.

I climbed out of bed.

"Where are you going?" asked the blond actress petulantly.

"To get some Scotch. You can have my wine."

I poured a strong drink into a big glass, took a long gulp, and returned to the bedroom. I climbed into bed and looked across the room at Sammy's picture.

Years were passing us by, I thought. Almost two years of acquiring friends the other knew nothing about, habits that would now appear strange to one another, memories that shouldn't be shared, thoughts that both of us couldn't be a party to.

196

Ah, but time heals.

Not always.

Sometimes it can reinjure, and sometimes it can lead a person into anger and pain he was unaware of before. Or if he was, perhaps now it was a different kind of anger and pain, a type that only time can ferment.

"Sammy would come back to you," said my sister, many months ago. "I'm sure of it, Tommy. I just know."

I thought so, too. I could tell in Sammy's letters, and in the tone of her voice on the telephone. I could tell when we met for dinner in New York, and when I came to her apartment to visit Carrie.

I could tell when a sudden funk would come out of nowhere, and I would react as if it were a reflex, and call Sammy immediately for aid and comfort. I could tell because she would give me aid and comfort.

Strange, then, that I didn't race back to her.

Why not?

Who *was* I racing to?

This stupid, insensate, lean-witted dolt lying next to me? This big-toothed buttercup watching television?

Jesus, Mother, Mary and Joseph.

"What the hell are you thinking about? You're so serious-looking," the blond actress said sharply. And then, in a swift change of pace, she draped herself across my chest and said, "Tell me. I'll understand," and she fluttered her false eyelashes and flashed her capped teeth.

"It's nothing," I said. "It's just a writing problem. You finish watching your television program. By the time it's over, I'll have it all figured out."

"Promise?"

"Promise," I said, and I thought of Sammy.

You would never leave me for another woman, would you? She had asked a long time ago.

No, I had answered.

Promise?

Promise.

And by the time the program's over, I'll have it all figured out.

"How long will you be in Europe this time?" my daughter had asked on the telephone a few days ago.

"I don't know," I lied. "Not very long."

"That's what you always say, Daddy, and then you stay a long time."

My daughter was eight now. I had missed two years of her life, and seemed destined to miss more.

"Hold on, Daddy. Mama wants to talk to you. But don't hang up when she's finished. I want to talk to you some more."

Sammy got on the telephone.

"Who are you going with?" she asked.

"Ellen." I hadn't asked Ellen yet, but I intended to.

Sammy put the telephone down. I could hear her crying in the background.

"Daddy," shouted my daughter, "what's the matter with Mama? She's crying. She's crying hard!"

Then my daughter started crying.

How often had I caused my daughter to cry?

"Daddy, please make Mama stop crying. Daddy, why is she crying so hard? Daddy, please come to New York right away! Please! *Please!*"

"I can't."

"Please!"

"I *can't,* Caroline."

"Please, Daddy! Please! Please come! Please!"

I heard my daughter crying until I hung up.

"The program's over!" chirped the blond actress. "I guess now's the time you stuff it in me, right?"

The next night I asked Ellen Harris to dinner.

We decided to eat at Martoni's restaurant, in Hollywood. It was after ten when we arrived, and the dinner crowd had thinned out. I requested a private booth in a corner, and that's where the headwaiter, Franco, sat us. Ellen slid in first and I started to sit beside her.

"Let's sit across from each other," she said.

"Why?" I asked. "We never sit across from each other. We always sit next to each other, and kiss and hug, and do things like that," I said, smiling.

"Please," she said softly, not smiling, "let's sit across from each other."

I knew then that Ellen Harris and I were through; finally and irrevocably through. I hadn't stopped playing my games in time.

I sat across from her.

I ordered drinks and felt a wretched, sad thickness spread in my chest and stomach. I hadn't felt a despondent ache like that, something having to do with love, or like, or whatever, for years.

She lit a cigarette.

"Well, Ellen," I said, bravely ignoring the signals, "we're finally going to do it. We're going to Europe, and we're going to stay there until I finish my book. Just the two of us. No friends, no enemies, no phonies, no fancy Hollywood parties, not even an occasional business meeting with a stockbroker. Nothing. Just you and me. We'll go to Saint Tropez. We'll get an apartment there. I know the place fairly well. And we'll stay as long as it takes: two weeks, two months, two years. It doesn't matter."

"Tommy . . ."

"Wait, Ellen. Let me finish."

I was selling hard, and my voice started to sound it.

"Ellen, no more games. No more fooling around. I'm tired of all that, I really am. I promise you I'm tired of all that."

And then I thought I heard myself begging, so I stopped.

Ellen just looked at her ashtray, and rotated it with her fingers. Where had I seen that before? And then I remembered. Mr. Wilkerson and his butter dish.

The waiter brought us our drinks.

"Ellen, I know I've promised this before, a dozen times, and I know you don't believe me, but *this* time it's true. Ellen, we love each other, and we need each other. We each fill a void the other has, and it's futile to fight it anymore. We've been tormenting each other for almost a year, and now it's all over. It's over, Ellen, once and for all."

Ellen Harris kept rotating her ashtray. She looked up at me and tears were running down her cheeks.

"Are you crying from happiness or sadness?" I asked. I knew the answer.

"From sadness," she said. "I'm not going with you, Tommy. I'm never going with you anywhere again. Ever."

She had said that before.

"You've said that before, Ellen."

"This time it's the truth," she said.

"Ellen, I *love* you."

"Maybe you do. Maybe in your sick, warped way you do. But I can't put up with you anymore. I just can't do it. You've set me up and knocked me down too many times, Tommy."

She wiped her eyes and put on sunglasses.

"Ellen," I said weakly, "the south of France."

"Tommy, a month ago I would have gone with you to Timbuktu, and you knew it. But now it's too late."

"Why? Why is it too late?"

"You know why. I'm dating someone, someone I like. I don't love him, but I like him. I never thought I could even *like* another man again. It's nice to know I can. I'm getting over you, Tommy. I'm surviving, and I'm glad."

I had met Ellen Harris in London. She had been skiing in Switzerland, and I was in Europe on one of my periodic quests for a place to write, a magic location that would bring me tranquillity, peace of mind, and an unexpected gush of creativity, instead of the loneliness and fallowness I was getting used to.

We were introduced at a small party in a mutual friend's apartment on Grosvenor Square. After the party, the two of us found a private club and drank there until they closed the place. I did everything I could to persuade Ellen Harris to come back to my hotel room. I thought I stood a chance. I was told she was a playgirl.

"What were you before you were a playgirl?" I had asked.

"I was a social butterfly. What were you before you were a millionaire?"

"Married," I answered, and that's when Ellen Harris first heard about Samantha Jane Wilkerson Christian.

I didn't take Ellen back to my hotel that night, but I did two nights later. We made love and it was fantastic.

We lived together in Malibu for two months, and then I threw her out.

"Why?" asked my sister.

"Because of Carrie," I had answered. "Carrie hates her, and I didn't think it was fair to impose that type of situation on a seven-year-old child."

"Well, I think you're nuts!" said Geraldine. "Sure your daughter hates her. She's jealous, and that's a perfectly natural reaction. But she'll be jealous of every woman you go out with, unless you handle the situation firmly, and unless you handle it *now*. You've got to nip this in the bud. Carrie must be made to understand that you love her more than anybody in the world *but* that her daddy has *his* life to live, too. Anyway, Carrie only sees you on holidays, so how bad can it be?"

"Well, she *is* my daughter, and—"

"Oh, *balls,*" interrupted Geraldine. "Stop reaching for excuses to run away from somebody you finally get to enjoy and are comfortable with. Ellen makes you happy, Tommy. She's young, and pretty, and smart, and you like being with her. I never saw you happier and more relaxed since you and Sammy broke up. Ellen is what you need, and that kind of woman is going to be very hard for you to find."

I walked the beaches by the cliffs for weeks, thinking about the things my sister had said. And then, one day, I decided that Geraldine was absolutely right.

When I called Ellen, she said she never wanted to see me again, but I talked her into it.

We saw each other steadily for three months, and then I felt trapped again. I started dating other girls, and flaunted them around town until Ellen found out.

She began going out with other men, stopping by my favorite places so that I could see who she was with. It made me furious.

When I couldn't bear it any longer, I called her and asked her out for dinner. We sat in a small booth in a dark corner. She looked down at her ashtray, and rotated it with her fingers.

She said that she never wanted to see me again, and that *this* time she was serious.

I told her that I couldn't stand knowing she was with other men, and that it drove me crazy to think that someone, other than I, might be sleeping with her. I told her that I had finally come to grips with the fact that I loved her. That I honestly, absolutely, and unquestionably loved her, and needed her.

She cried and put on her sunglasses.

She said that she would see me again *only* if I promised to stop playing games with her, once and for all.

I promised.

I didn't take out any other girls, but I didn't take Ellen out as often, either. I stayed home instead and tried working on my book. A week might pass before I would call Ellen, and when we talked, I had very little to say.

And then one weekend I missed Ellen very much, and suddenly realized how much I needed her. When I called her, she wasn't home. I tried her apartment every hour for the entire weekend, but there was no answer.

On Monday, when I finally reached her, I asked if we could have dinner. So, for the second time, Ellen Harris was sitting opposite me, wearing sunglasses and rotating an ashtray with her fingers.

"Ellen, I need you."

"I know you do," Ellen said. "And now I think even *you* know you do. But it's too late, and it's absurd. We can't win. I'll never be the number one woman in your life." I looked into her sunglasses and tried again.

"I know my daughter's been a problem for us," I said, "but I'm ready to cope with that problem. My sister and I were talking about that a long time ago. Geraldine said that Carrie has to get used to the fact that I have my own life to live. It's just taken me this long to understand that my sister was right."

"Your sister's *wrong!*" said Ellen, sitting straight up in her seat. She pushed her ashtray away. "It's *not* Carrie, for God's sake. It's *Sammy! That's* who's number one. Can't you get that through your head? Your daughter runs a poor second, and I'm not even in the race. Nobody is, and nobody ever will be. You're ruining your life not coming to grips with that fact, Tommy, and I'll be damned if you're going to ruin mine!"

She was crying again.

"Go back to her, Tommy. Go back to her, for Christ sake. Stop tearing yourself part. I'm mending. Let me mend. Please. Leave me alone. I've had enough of you, and I've had enough of her. I've had enough of her pictures, and her sayings, and her telephone calls, and the pressures she puts on you that I have to live with. I've had enough of your love for her—*not* for me, *for her!* I can't figure it out and I'm tired of trying to. I can't fight it anymore, Tommy. I can't." She turned to the wall and cried silently.

I watched her shoulders move up and down.

"Go back to her," she said, turning around. "Go back to her and give it another chance. You can't live without her. You're going to destroy yourself if you do."

I shook my head. "You're wrong, Ellen. I want *you.*"

"No."

"Please," I begged, "go with me to the south of France."

"No."

"Please. Just trust me this one last time."

"No."

"Please."

"No."

On the first day of May, Sammy called.

"I'm going to Europe the day after tomorrow," she said. "I think I'm going to take Carrie and move there as soon as school is over. I think that's where we'll live."

"Permanently?"

"Permanently," answered Sammy. "New York just isn't a summer festival anymore. You know, the smog, and the strikes every other day, and the crowds, and the crime. Wait a minute. I just want to get my cigarettes."

She went to get her cigarettes. She smokes too much, I thought to myself.

"Anyway," continued Sammy, "I'm not particularly in love with the schools here as much as I used to be, everything's too expensive, and I hate the mayor. I'm not so sure I'm that crazy about the governor, either, so maybe it's time for Carrie and me to take a sabbatical."

I slowly began to feel very sad and tired.

"Where will you go?" I asked.

"Geneva. I understand it's a very cosmopolitan city. Remember when we were there? We drove through Geneva on our way from Nice to Paris. I have some friends who live there. They've told me that the schools are excellent, and that the weather is fine. There's no industry in Geneva, so there's no smog at all. Also it's centrally located. It's less than an hour's flight to London, or Paris, or Copenhagen, or Rome. And it has a very international community. The United Nations is in Geneva, and so is the World Health Organization."

"You sound like a travelogue."

"Yes, I do, don't I?" said Sammy. "Anyway, I'm going over now, while there's still time before Carrie gets out of school. I'd like to see if I can find an apartment, and a summer camp nearby for Carrie. I also want to see if I can get Carrie into school. I understand it can be tough, so I want to take care of that, if I can."

"Who's going with you, the day after tomorrow?"

"Nobody," answered Sammy.

"I'll go along, if you want me to."

"Why?"

"I'm not sure why," I answered.

There was a pause, and then Sammy said, "Just you and me, babe?"

"Just you and me, babe."

"That would be fine," said Sammy.

The entire length of the hotel restaurant faced Lake Geneva. It was a large and ornate room. Had it been filled, there wouldn't have been any privacy. But that night, barely a dozen people sat in groups of various sizes at tables far apart from each other.

Sammy and I were seated at a table that was too large for us, behind a marble pillar. I walked to the window and looked at the lake. I heard Sammy order drinks. She asked for a Scotch and soda with a twist of lemon, and a glass of red wine.

The hotel was in a small town called Nyon, about a twenty-minute drive from Geneva. Almost every building in Nyon over-looked the lake. I watched the red and white pilot lights of a boat sail by, and then I went back to our table.

"Isn't this a beautiful dining room?" asked Sammy.

"Yes, it is," I answered, sitting down beside her.

We talked about the elegance of the hotel, and the charm of the village. We discussed the faces of the people sitting nearby, and the menu, and the waiters.

We talked to each other carefully. We were extra polite. We said excuse me, and pardon me, when we interrupted each other, and we laughed one or two seconds more than necessary when something funny was said.

We were nervous.

I turned my fork over and over, and Sammy ran her thumb and forefinger up and down her wineglass.

"Well," she said, "we've made it through a plane ride across the Atlantic, and an automobile ride from Geneva. And they said it would never last."

I laughed a little too long.

I rubbed her back and told her that she never *could* tell a joke.

"Very funny," she said, knocking me with her knee.

I leaned back in my chair and put my arm around her shoulders.

But it wasn't working.

Why wasn't it working? Why was I beginning to wish I wasn't there?

"It's nice to be together again," she said.

I didn't answer.

And then she put her face in her hands and began to cry.

Jesus, Mother, Mary and Joseph. I *knew* we would get to this, but I didn't think we would get to it so soon.

"What's the matter?" I asked.

"Nothing," Sammy said in gasps. "It's just that I wish we *were* together again. I want us to be together again so badly. All I want is a home and a family. I just want to take care of our house, and cook, and take care of our daughter, and sit by the fire while you write. I'm so lonely by myself. I'm so lonely."

I pulled my arm away from her shoulder and stared at my silverware.

"I'm sorry," she said, her face still in her hands. "I didn't mean to do this. I promised myself I wouldn't do this. I'm sorry." She took off her sunglasses and wiped her eyes with her napkin. "It's just that it's so horrible being a woman alone with a small child. It's horrible, and it's lonely, and it's awful. You shouldn't be living alone in California, and Carrie and I shouldn't be living without you in New York. We all should be living together. I can't stand the loneliness anymore, Tommy. I really can't."

Sammy wiped her eyes again.

"I've been thinking about us ever since you sold your company. I never thought you really would, but you did. Now we have time to smell flowers again, like you used to say. And you're writing again. It's what we were waiting for. It's like it used to be. I don't have to live a memory anymore. We never stopped loving each other, Tommy. Let's not stop now."

"Sammy, honey, please," I said. I felt embarrassed and uncomfortable. Our waiter came toward us, turned, and walked away.

"I'm sorry, Tommy," she said. "It's just all coming out, and I can't stop it."

"Sammy," I said quietly, "it's not doing you *or* me any good. You know we can't go back together. It's impossible. It just wouldn't work. Four or five days in Geneva isn't the same as living together, day in and day out. We just have to go on living that memory. We have no other choice. Times have changed, but our problems together haven't. Unfortunately we still have our differences, and those differences make it impossible for us to go back. Oh, maybe we could fool each other for a week, or a month, or maybe six months, but sooner or later we'd fall apart again."

"*What* differences?" asked Sammy, looking directly at me.

"What differences? Me. My friends. My life style. Ever since I became successful, you've hated everything about me."

"I have not," she said softly.

"Well, it's too late," I said, feeling a rage bristling about me. "It's too late. And besides, I'm too angry. I have too much hurt and pain in me. I loved you *too* much. *Too much!* I loved you so much, I can't get the hurt and anger out of my system. I've tried. God knows I've tried."

I took a deep breath, and a gulp of my drink. I was trying to control myself.

"Sammy, I've thought so much about us, I'm tired of thinking. I just want you to go your way and I'll go mine. I just want to live as simply as I can, and get a small amount of love and companionship from someone, but that someone can't be you. It's too late for that someone to be you!"

I felt the rage flaring up again.

"I took you when you were a mess and loved you until you became whole again. I took you when you had twitches, and asthma, and bottles of vodka in every other drawer, and I loved you and cared for you. You were a goddamned basket case, and I loved you anyway. And I never *stopped* loving you and I don't know if I ever will. And I worked my ass off to make something for both of us and I succeeded, and what did I get from you? What did I get? I'll tell you what I got. I got a big, fat, fucking kick in the ass, that's what I got.

"You should have thought about the consequences *before* you ran around with your goddamn painter or whoever you ran around with in Mexico. You should have thought about the goddamn loneliness and all of that shit *then.* Now it's too late.

"We can't go back together again, Sammy. We *can't.* You know why? I'll tell you why. Because I'll never be able to sleep with you again. *Never!* I'll think of that rotten fucking painter and I'll never be able to sleep with you. You blew it, Sammy. You just goddamn blew it. I loved you like nobody will *ever* love you, and you blew it."

I was fuming, and I didn't care if the entire restaurant heard me. I was too mad to care.

"Bullshit!" said Sammy. She wasn't crying anymore. She was sitting back in her chair, perfectly composed. "You're lying, Tommy. You're absolutely wrong. It's not your great love for me that's eating your heart out. It's not this dramatic anger and hurt you can't get out of your beloved system that's screwing you all up. It's your ego! Your gigantic, tremendous, super ego. That's what it is, and you're not man enough to swallow it!"

Sammy took a sip of her wine, turned, and looked me right in the eyes. "My stupid father was right," she said. "You *are* an opportunist! You're a selfish egotist, and all opportunists are selfish egotists. You're selfish, self-indulgent, self-centered, self-serving, self, self, self. You don't care about me *or* your daughter. You don't care about your mother, or your sister, or what the hell's happening in the world. You just care about yourself. Your whole life is centered around Thomas C. Christian. I could come to you on my *knees* and you wouldn't forgive me. I could nail myself to a goddamn cross and you wouldn't forgive me. You *can't*. I hurt your *ego!* I hurt your *pride!* And you'll *never* be able to forgive me for doing that. You are incapable of forgiveness, Tommy, especially when it comes to your ego. You're a cripple, Tommy. You're an emotional cripple, and I feel sorry for you."

We drove back to Geneva in silence.

That night, when Sammy fell asleep, I decided to write her a letter and leave.

She would have a car. She had friends in Geneva. She had plenty of money with her. And hadn't she planned to go alone in the first place?

As soon as I finished the letter, I would go to the airport and take the first plane out. It didn't matter to me in the slightest where it was going.

It took me over two hours to write the letter. Every now and then I would walk into the bedroom of our suite and check on Sammy. She tossed and turned, but never woke up. When I finished the letter, I folded it and put it in an envelope. I licked the envelope closed and propped it up on the desk under a big lamp. I had written SAMMY on the front of the envelope in big block letters.

SAMMY, in big block letters, under a lamp in a Geneva hotel. The end.

I flopped into a large, heavily carved armchair. I looked across the room at the envelope that had SAMMY written on it. I don't know how long I stared at that envelope, but eventually I went back to the desk, ripped the letter into tiny pieces, threw the pieces into the wastebasket, and went to sleep next to Sammy.

Sammy and I managed to live peacefully together for the next eight days and nights. We fell into a sort of truce, brought on by the mutual knowledge that we were capable of hurting each other enormously.

So we had a good time instead.

Sammy found an apartment, and the two of us spoke to the headmaster of the International School about Carrie.

"How would you describe your daughter?" asked the headmaster.

"A basic pain in the ass," answered Sammy.

"Honey!" I exclaimed.

"Well, how would *you* describe your daughter?" asked Sammy.

"As a basic pain in the ass," I agreed, "but a smart one. Our daughter's a very *bright* pain in the ass," I said to the headmaster.

He smiled. He was a nice man, I think.

We walked through the streets of Geneva, window-shopping. Once in a while, we bought each other something. I bought Sammy a pennant that said GENEVA, SWITZERLAND, and Sammy bought me a soft-boiled egg thing that takes off the top of the eggshell neatly.

"Something I've always wanted," I said.

"You should be eating soft-boiled eggs now," she said. "You're not a kid anymore, you know." She wasn't smiling, either. I think she really thought I should be eating soft-boiled eggs.

We sat at outdoor cafés and ate ice cream, and we walked along the lake, peeking into houseboats that were docked in the marina. We dined in the finest restaurants, and in *the* finest restaurant in Geneva I got very drunk, and Sammy had to drag me out, drive us home, and put me to bed.

"How come you got so drunk last night?" she asked in the morning.

"I don't know," I answered. "It just seemed to happen."

"You kissed me and hugged me a lot," Sammy said. "You should get drunk more often."

210

One day we got a telegram from my sister Geraldine. She and her husband were arriving in Montreux the next day and they wanted us to meet them there.

I called the hotel my sister was coming to and made a reservation. We left early the next morning and took the long route to Montreux, through Coppet, Morges, Lausanne, and Vevey. It was a beautiful drive. We stopped for lunch five or six times, and we rarely passed a patisserie without pulling over so that one of us could run in and buy a few assorted goodies.

When we arrived at the hotel in Montreux, there was a wire waiting for us.

"What's it say?" asked Sammy.

"My sister's not coming. She's had a change of plans. She says that we should kiss each other for her."

We kissed each other and drove back to Geneva.

And then one day there was nothing else to do; no reason to stay in Europe any longer. It was time to go home.

Sammy was going back to New York.

I didn't know what to do.

"What will you do?" asked Sammy.

"I don't know. If I go to New York or Los Angeles, I'll get involved with boring stockbrokers who still bother me with business propositions that drive me right out of my mind. And if I stay here I'll be lonely. It's six of one, half a dozen of another, I guess."

"Poor Thomas," said Sammy, with genuine concern.

That night, at dinner, I told Sammy I had decided to go home to Malibu. "Be it ever so humble, and all that crap," I mumbled to my knife and fork.

"I'm glad," she said. "I'd hate to think of you wandering about Europe all by yourself."

We agreed to fly back from Paris. That way, I could take a plane nonstop to Los Angeles. We also decided to drive from Geneva to Paris. Sammy and I had done that before, many years ago.

At that time we were on our way home to New York. I had just finished my book, and we were traveling to Paris to spend three inexpensive days celebrating. We drove an old but hardy Citroën, and we were very much in love.

The Citroën was a dull gray, and it didn't have a gas gauge. You measured its needs by poking a stick down its fuel tank. I used to run out of gas a lot, but somehow it seemed funny then.

You could also pull the Citroën's front seat out of the car and use it as a chair. Actually, the front seat was more like a hammock than a front seat. It was ideal for sitting under full, green, over-hanging trees and on soft grassy hillsides, which Sammy and I did at every opportunity. We would sit on that absurd front seat and fill ourselves with wine and cheese, and kisses and hugs. It was nice.

Nine years ago we stopped for mustard in Dijon. While we were there, we sat at an outdoor café and talked about having a baby. The next night, in Paris, we took a hot bath together in a deep tiled tub. Later Sammy cried and I wasn't sure why. She said she was crying because she was happy.

Later in bed we made a child.

She would be a girl with a peaches-and-cream complexion, green eyes, and blond hair. She would have a lot to say, her name would be Caroline, and everyone would agree that she looked like me.

And now, nine years later, Sammy and I would be driving through Dijon and into Paris again.

We left early the next morning and drove through fresh, lovely countryside, sometimes Swiss, sometimes French. The route twisted back and forth across the border.

When we were in France once and for all, we stopped at a patisserie and bought two fragile napoleons. We ate them in the car and got crumbs and powdered sugar all over our laps.

We had lunch in Lons-le-Saunier, and stopped for mustard again in Dijon. I watched Sammy through the window of the mustard shop. She was discussing prices with the crotchety old-maid owner of the store. Sammy enjoyed haggling with shop-keepers, and claimed the shopkeepers liked it, too.

"They love it," she would say. "It makes their day complete."

Often I tended to doubt her. The crotchety mustard lady didn't seem to be loving it at all.

I walked inside the shop and followed my wife up and down several aisles. When I had the opportunity, I told her not to be so hard on the old lady.

"She loves it," she said, never taking her eyes off the various jars of mustard. "This will absolutely make her day complete."

I trailed her for a while, then I wandered off by myself.

I looked in a few store windows and ultimately bought a soft ice cream cone and a silly blue peaked seaman's cap.

Before we left Dijon, we had a glass of red wine at a café.

"Do you think this is the same café we sat in the last time we were here?" asked Sammy.

"I don't think so," I answered, but it might have been.

We walked back to the car. Every time we crossed a street, Sammy held my hand.

It started to rain heavily and the roadway became slick and slippery. Cars went whizzing past us, splashing water on our windshield. We passed a grisly automobile accident just out-side of Villeneuve. It was on the other side of the highway. A car was overturned and several people were lying along the side of the road. An ambulance stood nearby with its red light turning. Every automobile stopped to look, and then went off again, somewhat slower than before. I told Sammy that I was beginning to feel jumpy, so we pulled into a gas station–restaurant for coffee.

I went to the men's room and washed. I looked in the mirror and studied my face. I wasn't impressed.

As I walked back to our table, I could see across the room that Sammy was crying. She didn't see me, so I waited until she composed herself.

When I sat down, Sammy poured me a cup of coffee. "You know, Tommy," she said, "you are a horse's ass."

I wanted to ask why, but I didn't.

"Because you *are*," she said, as if I had asked.

We were lost in Paris, and took lefts and rights at random until we miraculously found ourselves on the Left Bank, just three blocks from our hotel. We looked at each other and smiled.

I turned off the Boulevard Saint Germain and parked in front of the Hotel des Saints-Pères. It was our favorite hotel in Paris. Sammy and I had sat in one of its deep tiled bathtubs nine years ago and laughed and cried.

The night clerk said there were no rooms.

We went up the Rue des Saints-Pères to another hotel, and were told that we could be accommodated for just one night. You could only get to the room by taking the elevator up three flights, and walking down two. Or you could walk up.

Later, we sat at the Café Deux Magots and watched the people go by. I drank Pernod because that's what Hemingway drank when he sat at the Café Deux Magots.

"Did you ever check out whether Hemingway *really* drank Pernod when he sat here?" asked Sammy.

"No."

"Well, you should."

"Why?" I asked.

"Because you *hate* the stuff," she answered.

We walked up the Boulevard Saint Germain and passed a man selling crêpes from a cart. The smell was fantastic, and even though we had just had dinner, we bought two. He put a lot of sugar and rum on them, rolled them up, and handed them to us like ice cream cones.

Before we went to bed, I asked Sammy if she had everything. She said she did.

"Your plane ticket?"

"Yes."

"Your passport?"

"Yes."

"Let me give you some extra cash," I said, "just in case anything unusual happens."

"Why, Thomas," she said, in a singsong voice, "you'll say just *any*thing to get me in bed with you."

"Very funny," I said, and we went to sleep, or at least we tried.

I stayed awake for a while listening to the sounds of the hotel: a flushing toilet, someone coming up the creaking steps, the elevator doors opening and closing. A woman was talking on the telephone and her voice echoed around the courtyard. A man in another room yelled at her to be quiet.

Sometime during the night I finally fell asleep.

Neither of us had much of an appetite for breakfast. I fingered my brioche, and the coffee tasted horrible.

We hardly spoke, driving to the airport. When we got there, Sammy got out and I parked the car. I thought about turning in the car keys and the rental papers, changed my mind, and joined Sammy by the departure board.

We had a cup of coffee until it was time for her to go, and then I walked Sammy to her gate. She went through the turnstile and came back to me. She stood on the other side of the railing.

"Can I ask you something?" she said.

"Sure. What?"

"Are we ever going to see each other again?"

"I don't know."

"You mean no more trips, or anything like that?"

"I don't know, Sammy."

"Not even an occasional movie?" she asked.

"I don't know."

"Yes you do," she said, and then she picked up her handbags and walked away.

I woke at dawn.

A group of dogs were howling down the street, as if something terrible was about to take place. I had read somewhere that a concert of howling dogs was a forecast of imminent doom, so I stayed in bed, hardly breathing, waiting for their prediction to come true. When nothing happened, I got up, dressed, and went outside.

Today is beginning like all the days have begun for the last three weeks: gray, damp, and sunless. The tide is out, leaving a new supply of shells and debris on the sand. The straits are rough, and the trees along the shore bend and flap from the strong, cold sea wind.

This morning I put on two sweaters under my topcoat, but I was still chilly. It's hard to believe it's June.

But then who cares what month it is?

I don't.

Nothing seems to matter. I don't feel like doing anything. I have no desire to go home, yet it seems pointless to stay in Calais. I just spend my time walking along this dreary, bleak French coastline, watching sea gulls and examining driftwood.

Yesterday I walked for hours. It must have been nearly noon when I finally got back to my room. And now I'm going along the same path again, passing the same sea gulls, and the same pieces of wood.

Last night I didn't sleep well. While I lay in bed, I thought of a poem I used to recite to my daughter. I turned on my back and said it out loud to the ceiling.

> Where am I going? I don't quite know.
> Down the stream where the kingcups grow.
> Up the hill where the pine trees blow.
> Anywhere, anywhere. I don't know.
>
> Where am I going? The high rocks call:
> "It's awful fun to be born at all."

Where am I going? The ring doves coo:
"We do have beautiful things to do."

Where am I going? I don't quite know.
What does it matter where people go?
Down to the woods where the bluebells grow.
Anywhere, anywhere. I don't know.

Today is my birthday. Happy birthday, Tommy.